A LUSTY CHALLENGE

"I may be honorable, but I'm not soft in the head," Avril told him.

Brandr half-smiled. "You look soft to me."

Her composure slipped, but only for an instant. "I assure you, you wouldn't be the first man I sent limping from the field of battle."

His eyes narrowed suggestively. "And you wouldn't be the first woman I laid out flat on her back."

THE SHIPWRECK

Cover photo courtesy of Armstreet, makers of medieval clothing, www.armstreet.com. If you like the outfit, you can own it!
Cover design by Richard Campbell
Formatting by Author E.M.S.

Glynnis Campbell – Publisher
P.O. Box 341144
Arleta, California 91331
ISBN-10: 1938114272
ISBN-13: 978-1-938114-27-4
Contact: glynnis@glynnis.net

Published in the United States of America.

The Shipwreck

The Prequel Novella to
The Warrior Maids of Rivenloch

For Birthe Hansen,
my dear friend and rowing partner
on the Viking longship adventure

CHAPTER 1

The Ninth Century,
Off the Eastern Coast of Pictland

The last ominous sound Brandr heard, before the icy ocean closed over his head, blocking out the roar of the storm and the crash of the waves, was the deep crack of his longship splitting apart.

The current dragged at his sealskin cloak and boots, pulling him down. But with his one still useful arm, he managed to claw his way to the surface. Gasping frosty air into his lungs as he broke through the waves, he blinked back the stinging saltwater, trying to see in the relentless black night. The ship's lanterns had gone out. No light came from the distant shore. Even the trusty stars were hidden behind thunderheads.

"Erik!" he bellowed. "Erik! Gunnarr! Haral—"

A gulp of seawater choked off his cries. He fought to stay

afloat in the paralyzing cold, turning in the water, listening for his shipmates. But all he could hear was the howl of the wind, the pounding of the sea, and the splintering of wood as his ship was dashed against the rocks.

A flash of lightning split the sky, zigzagging down like Thor's avenging spear to blacken the timber of the mast. Before Brandr could wonder what he'd done to offend the god, thunder rocked the heavens, and the top of the mast exploded into sparks, igniting the square sail. For a moment it looked as if the dragon painted on the canvas was breathing fire.

By the light of the flaming sail, Brandr could see the extent of the damage to his ship. The hull was broken. Ropes snapped wildly in the shrieking wind. Chests and oars slid into the sea. And his crew...

Shuddering with cold and pain, fighting the tide, he called over the roaring of the storm until he was hoarse. He found four of his men. They were dead.

The rain eventually arrived to extinguish the fiery wreckage. Brandr—beaten by the storm, devastated by loss, and too exhausted to care what happened to him—used the last of his strength to climb atop the splintered prow of his ship and resigned himself to the whim of the gods.

Death was following him. It had already come for his wife and children. Now it had come for his men. Soon it would come for him. And as far as Brandr was concerned, it could have him.

"Stay close!" Avril called after Kimbery, shaking her head as the four-year-old raced ahead of her across the wet sand. Her intrepid daughter possessed insatiable curiosity, incurable wanderlust, and a stubborn will that left her deaf to her mother's warnings.

Not that there was much to warn her about. Here in their seaside home, they lived far out of everyone's way. No one would stumble across their stone cottage or cross their stretch of beach by accident. Their exile to the eastern shores had left them in a location that was remote, isolated...and far enough from her ancestral home of Rivenloch to satisfy the brothers who'd stolen it from her.

In the distance, Kimbery squealed as she bent over some treasure along the tide's edge—probably a pretty shell or a starfish washed ashore in last night's storm. Avril kicked off her boots and hefted up her basket. With any luck, the wild tempest had stirred up something edible from the sea.

The brothers who'd banished her had probably expected her to starve, her and her "bastard Viking spawn," as they called Kimbery. Certainly, her death would have been convenient for them.

But Avril hadn't obliged them.

As willful as her daughter, she'd persisted, refusing to die. The land was hostile to crops, but she'd adapted to it. She'd learned to fish, to dig for clams, to pry mussels from rock, to snare coneys, to raid seagull nests, to make broth from seaweed and pottage from oysters. She'd even traded a silver cloak pin to her closest neighbor for a ewe that had lost its lamb, so she had milk, butter, cheese, and wool for clothing. A stream emptied into the ocean a short distance from the cottage, giving her ample water for drinking and bathing, and trout for supper.

But none of it was easy. So when the weather turned violent as it had last night and the ocean's belly roiled, spewing its contents onto the beach, Avril considered it a gift from the sea. She might find a few stranded fish not yet picked apart by the gulls, a sizable clump of kelp, a useful shell, or even an odd tool or bit of line lost from a fishing boat.

Kimbery, of course, was convinced she'd unearth a mermaid's jewels or Poseidon's trident or an otter to keep for a pet. She'd learned to relish the flash of lightning and the crack of thunder that foretold a day of treasure-hunting on the beach.

The wee lass didn't know any different. But Avril was well aware of how wrong their life of scraping and scavenging was. If she thought too deeply about what had been taken from her—her maidenhood, her lands, a proper family and playmates for her daughter, and about the fact that she'd been groomed from birth, not to dwell in a hovel, but to command a sizable holding—she'd be filled with constant rage and an unquenchable thirst for vengeance.

But there was nothing she could do. Invading Northmen had left her with child and killed her father. And once he was dead, her four younger brothers, racked with jealousy over the favoritism their father had shown her as the rightful heir, declared Avril unfit to rule Rivenloch. All the years her father had spent training her to take over his command—schooling her in the law, teaching her to wield a sword, bringing her up to be a moral, fair, honest leader—had been wasted. She was sent into exile with her daughter and what little she could carry on her back. And not a soul in Rivenloch had had the courage to face her thieving brothers and come forward in her defense.

Still, not a day passed that she didn't think about winning it all back. It was only concern for her daughter's welfare that kept Avril from taking up her sword and marching boldly to the gates of Rivenloch to demand the return of her keep.

"Mama!" Kimbery cried, draping a piece of dark seaweed over her sun-bright curls and skipping along the sea foam. "I'm a selkie!"

She smiled. She often wondered if ocean-loving Kimbery might indeed be half-seal. It was the little girl's inventiveness that kept her own bitterness at bay and kept her fighting for survival. Sometimes Avril thought that being impregnated by a Viking berserker was the best thing that had ever happened to her.

She scanned the rocky tidepools as she walked toward the ocean, searching for periwinkles, glancing occasionally up at Kimbery to be sure she wasn't straying too far. The wee lass had a healthy respect for the sea, but the tide could be unpredictable and unforgiving.

The air was calm today, and the sky was an unchanging gray, but evidence of the storm littered the beach. Avril picked up a piece of driftwood and poked at a clump of kelp on the sand. A fat abalone was attached to one of the strands, and it would make a nice supper tonight. She cut it loose, plopping it into her basket. A small purple starfish with six legs was stuck to the kelp, too. Though it was inedible, she added it to the basket to show to Kimbery, knowing she'd like its color. Closer to the water, she found a few crabs, but their shells had been picked clean by the seabirds.

She glanced up. Kimbery was hunkered down beside a tiny crab on the sand, and when the tide rushed in to cover it, the lass shrieked and leaped up, running and giggling as the ocean chased her.

Avril was still grinning when her attention was caught by something floating off the rocky point that jutted into the sea. It looked like a substantial piece of wood, maybe a crate or part of a cart, something that might prove useful. As she gradually made her way toward the point, she collected a few mussels for pottage and a large clamshell suitable for a bowl.

"Mama!"

Avril narrowed her eyes at the wood bobbing in the water. What was it? Though one end appeared to be splintered, the other sides were finished. Maybe it was a broken chest or a table.

"Mama! Look what I found!"

"In a moment!" she called back, studying the piece as it was tossed by the current.

"Mama! It's my da!"

That got her attention. Avril whipped her head around and peered down the shoreline to where Kimbery was squatting beside a furry bulk on the sand.

It looked like a dead seal.

"See, Mama?"

Of course, Avril realized—Kimbery was pretending she was a selkie, so the dead seal must be her da. The lass had a vivid imagination. "I see!" A seal was indeed a good find. If it was freshly killed, its meat could keep their bellies full a long while. And she could make coats and slippers out of its fur. "I'll be right there! Don't touch it!"

A few more yards and she'd get a good look at whatever was floating off the point. If it wasn't worth salvaging, she'd leave it be and see what she could get off the dead seal.

A broad wave caught the wood and turned it on its side. The instant she saw the design, her heart dropped to the pit of her stomach. A great round knob rose above the water. Painted on its surface in hues of red and blue was the face of a snarling dragon. It was the masthead of a longship.

Time slowed as she dropped her basket and turned toward Kimbery.

"Nay!" she screamed.

She picked up her skirts and tried to race across the beach, but the air suddenly felt heavy, and the sand dragged at her heels. Kimbery seemed impossibly distant and far too close to the body that Avril could see now was not a dead seal, but the remains of a man.

The bloody images of the berserker attack were as clear and fresh as that day five years ago...

Wild-eyed, axe-wielding giants bursting through the

gates of Rivenloch, roaring and foaming at the mouth, hacking at everything in their path, smashing pottery, splitting furniture, slicing flesh...

The hounds' yelps, cut off abruptly as their throats were slit...

The steward falling as his legs were cut out from under him...

A shrieking serving woman losing her arm...

One fleeing child axed in the back while another was trampled beneath heavy boots...

A young lass, frozen with fear, snatched up and carried off, never to be seen again...

It was happening again. The Northmen had returned. Avril staggered onto one knee.

Then she looked up at Kimbery, still yards away, and bit out a curse. She wouldn't let the bastards have her daughter. She was no longer the innocent lass she'd been five years ago who'd become a victim of rape. She was prepared for them this time. Clenching her jaw in determination, she scrambled to her feet again and hurtled forward across the sand.

At last she reached Kimbery, sweeping her into her arms and clutching her so tightly that the wee lass squealed in complaint.

"Shh!" She spun, searching the boulders and clumps of sea grass lining the shore. The longship must have crashed in the storm. But what had become of its crew? Where were the dead man's shipmates?

Everything seemed normal, undisturbed. Waves lapped at the beach, leaving arcs of foam. Gulls screed

and soared overhead. Crabs skittered over the rocks. No strange footprints marred the virgin stretch of sand.

"Mama," Kimbery whimpered impatiently. "Put me down."

"Hush." Avril scoured the beach once more. The Vikings had come again. There was no mistaking the origin of the carved dragon's head. But they weren't here now. Either they'd bypassed her cottage and moved inland already, or their dead bodies would be washing ashore soon. But for now at least, it appeared she and Kimbery were safe.

"Maaaamaaa," Kimbery whined.

She let Kimbery slip to the ground. The lass immediately skipped over to the dead man.

"Don't touch him," Avril repeated.

Kimbery crouched a few feet away from him, resting her elbows on her knees and her chin in her hands, peering curiously into his face. "Is it my da?"

"Nay!" Avril replied, a little too vehemently, though she could see why the lass would think that. The man's face was hidden behind strands of long blond hair that was the same pale color as Kimbery's. He was covered in a cloak of seal fur, and his sealskin boots looked much like theirs. But there the resemblance ended. He was a giant, a head taller than any man she knew. His shoulders were broad and his feet huge. A silver cuff in a dragon design encircled one thick wrist, and hanging around his wide neck from a leather thong was a hammer of silver with foreign runes carved into it.

Thank God he was dead. His kind—the invaders from

the North—were bloodthirsty, vicious, ruthless murderers.

She shuddered. Despite the value of all that silver, she had no desire to loot the corpse. She didn't want to touch a Viking at all. Then she frowned in distaste. What *would* she do with the body? She didn't want it rotting on her shore. She'd have to bury it, she supposed. It was a pity it *wasn't* a beached seal. That much meat would have seen them through the winter.

Kimbery, flouting Avril's instructions, picked up a club of driftwood and began nudging the man's bloody shoulder. Avril shook her head. The lass might not openly disobey her by touching the dead man, but even at four years old, she had an annoying habit of stretching the rules as far as she could.

"Wake up!" the lass shouted into his unresponsive face.

"He's dead, Kimmie."

"Nay, he's not."

"Aye, he is," she said, though Kimbery's yelling was fit to wake the dead.

Kimbery curled her determined lip and nudged him again.

Avril raised a sardonic brow. Maybe she *could* cook him up for supper. There was probably a few hundred pounds of muscle on his large frame.

Then again, Viking meat was probably tough and foul-tasting.

"Wake! Up!" Kimbery punctuated each word with a hard poke of her driftwood.

"Kimbery, leave the poor—"

Then he groaned.

Avril froze. Shite. Kimbery was right. He wasn't dead.

"See, Mama? I told you he was—"

She snatched the lass up so fast, the little girl's head snapped backward.

The man groaned again. Avril snagged the driftwood out of Kimbery's hand and held it in front of her like a weapon.

Then Kimbery began to wail, which caused the man to rouse.

"Sh-sh-sh-sh-sh." Avril bounced the lass on her left hip, hoping to quiet her, to no avail. Damn! What would she do if the man regained consciousness? She wished she'd brought her sword. He'd swat away her driftwood club as easily as a piece of straw.

She could run. If she hurried, she could make it to her cottage with Kimbery before the man found his feet. But that would only delay him. Eventually he'd come and knock down her door, probably with one solid punch of his oversized fist.

Kimbery, enraged at being thwarted and oblivious to the danger, squirmed out of Avril's grip just as the man's eyes fluttered open.

"Run!" she screamed at Kimbery, who was already tearing off toward the cottage in fury.

Avril turned back to the man. She just glimpsed the ice-blue hue of his opening eyes before she swung around with the driftwood, clubbing him in the head as hard as she could.

CHAPTER 2

Avril was glad Kimbery hadn't witnessed her mother clouting a helpless castaway.

She winced as she used the pointy end of the driftwood to cautiously sweep aside the unconscious man's hair. Blood trickled down his temple where she'd struck him, but his pulse still beat steadily in his throat.

Thank God she hadn't killed him. True, Northmen were degenerate and insidious and evil. But slaying an unarmed man went against everything her father had taught her about honor.

Now what was she going to do with him? He might wake again at any moment. She couldn't keep clubbing him. But she had to keep him subdued. And she had to get him out of sight.

She didn't really want him in her home, but she didn't have much of a choice. She couldn't afford to have him roaming loose. At least in the cottage, she could keep her eye on him.

Dropping the driftwood, she separated out one long strand of tough kelp caught on his boot and wrapped it around his ankles several times. She wrapped another thick strand around his wrists, noting that his left forearm was bruised and swollen.

She scowled. It looked like he'd broken his arm. Then she remembered he was the enemy and it didn't matter to her if he'd broken his arm. She only hoped the bonds would hold until she reached the cottage and could tie him up with something more substantial.

Dragging him up the beach by his ankles was harder than she expected. His legs were leaden, and in his waterlogged clothing, he was as heavy as a walrus. With every backward step, the wet sand sucked at her feet, hampering her progress.

Halfway up the shore, she stopped to rest. Kimbery was safe now. She'd slammed the door behind her, and Avril could hear the little girl's muffled wailing coming from inside the cottage.

While she caught her breath, Avril wiped the sweat from her forehead and took a moment to study her captive. A light growth of beard covered his chin, but he looked considerably younger than the savage who'd raped her five years ago. His face was not unhandsome. His skin was darkened by the sun and salted by the sea, but he lacked the heavy lines of age. His nose was straight, his cheekbones were unbroken, and his brow was strong. If his size didn't give him away, the brief glimpse of his bright blue eyes confirmed he was a Northman.

She blew out a long breath and looked out to sea. In the distance, she could see refuse bobbing atop the waves and drifting toward the shore. Soon, splinters of his ship would make landfall, along with broken oars, bits of rigging, and, she thought with a shudder, the waterlogged corpses of his shipmates.

It took every bit of Brandr's willpower to play dead. He still couldn't believe the sweet-faced maiden had clubbed him with a cudgel of driftwood. But he didn't want her to club him again, not while he didn't have the strength to fight her. So he remained quiet as she began dragging him across the sand.

His head throbbed where she'd hit him, his muscles ached, and the deep-seated, dull pain in his left forearm told him he'd probably broken it.

It was still his heart that hurt the most. In the past year, he'd lost everything...his wife, his children, his ship, his men. It must be some cruel trick of the gods to keep him alive to endure such anguish.

After a while, the woman, panting heavily from her exertions, dropped his feet onto the sand and stopped to catch her breath. Even with his eyes closed, he could feel her gaze upon him like the searing touch of the sun.

What did she intend? She must not mean to kill him. Otherwise, he'd be dead by now. He figured he was somewhere along the Pictish coast, though he wasn't sure where or how he'd washed ashore. Until he got his

bearings and regained his strength, he was better off feigning unconsciousness.

Which was even more challenging when the woman resumed dragging him, this time up a stone pathway and over the threshold of a cottage, jarring his ribs and banging his skull on the hard rock.

At least it was warm indoors. He thought his bones would never thaw. He heard the comforting crackle of a fire and smelled pottage simmering on the hearth. And then he heard something that wrenched at his memory—the quiet sobbing of a child.

Unbidden, the faces of Sten and Asta appeared in his mind's eye, and unbearable pain seized him as he realized he'd never see his children or his wife Inga again. The last time he'd seen them alive was when he'd set sail on a raiding voyage with his brothers, Ragnarr and Halfdan. By the time he returned, his family had been dead two months, stolen from him by a sickness that had swept through the village. His brothers' families had succumbed as well, and even though they'd never said so, he was sure his brothers regretted going on that last long raid with him.

"Shh, Kimmie, it's all right now," the woman murmured in Pictish. It was a language Brandr had learned as a boy from the slaves his father had brought home.

"You hurt me," the little girl sobbed.

"I didn't mean to hurt you, wee one," the woman replied. "But I'm very proud of you for running home. You did just the right thing. You were very brave. And you ran very fast."

The pain in Brandr's chest deepened. The woman might speak a different language, but her motherly voice reminded him of his precious Inga.

The little girl came closer, her voice hitching with spent tears. "Will my...my da...live with us now?"

"He's not your da."

"He is."

"Nay."

"Aye."

"Nay, he's not," the mother replied testily as she began cutting the bonds around his ankles. "Why do you keep saying that?"

"He *is* my da. He *is*," the little girl insisted, starting to cry again.

"Kimmie, I've told you a hundred times. Your da is dead."

"That's what you said about *him*." Brandr imagined the little girl was sticking out a pouty lip the way Asta always did when she knew she was right.

The woman, unable to come up with a suitable reply, changed the subject. "Look in the chest beside the bed and see if you can find Finn's leash."

Leash. Leash? That didn't bode well. What was she up to?

He didn't find out until it was too late. As she started sawing at the kelp bonds around his wrists, she wrenched his broken arm, and the pain was so severe that he blacked out.

When Brandr awoke again, he was bound in a leather collar and leashed tightly by his neck through an iron ring attached to the wall. His sealskin cloak was missing, leaving him sitting in his tunic, trousers, and boots. His bound legs stretched nearly to the hearth, his arms were secured to his sides by a rope around his midsection, and his wrists were tied before him.

Fury surged through his veins. By Thor! He'd come here to conquer, not to be conquered. How could he have wound up a prisoner—the prisoner of a woman?

While his rage simmered, he perused the room through narrowed eyelids. His cloak had been hung on a peg near the fire. And his captors supped at a table across the chamber, unaware that he'd roused.

He could see why the little girl thought he was her father. They shared the same blond hair. The girl was younger than his daughter, but in her dust-colored kirtle and bare feet, she reminded him of Asta.

Though he hated to admit it, the mother was breathtaking. Her hair, an intoxicating color of golden mead and ruby wine combined, hung in thick waves down her back, and her skin was as golden and radiant as flame. Her face was artfully sculpted, with generous lips and finely arched brows, and her snugly-laced, faded blue kirtle revealed pleasing womanly curves.

But this was the same lovely temptress who'd clubbed him, dragged him home, and tied him up like a dog. He wasn't about to be fooled by her pretty face.

He studied the stone cottage, which was well-kept and welcoming. Its curious furnishings appeared to be made mostly of scavenge from the sea. Odd pieces of driftwood were fitted together to form stools, and candles were set in holders made of mussel shells. A bit of fishing net tacked onto one wall held hair combs carved out of abalone, and on a shelf fashioned out of an oar sat an assortment of clamshell bowls and dishes. A fishing pole and a net were propped against the hearth. But it was what was leaned against the corner that interested him most.

It was a nobleman's sword, a magnificent blade. Its pommel was set with gems, the grip was wrapped in seasoned leather, and the guard was carved with designs that intersected, weaving complex knots. The sword looked well cared for. The steel was highly polished, the edge keen. He wondered where the man who owned the weapon was.

"Mama," the little girl said, picking up her clamshell bowl, "my da wants some, too."

"He's not your da, Kimmie, and he's not even..." She ended on a gasp as she glanced his way.

It was too late to feign sleep.

She rose suddenly, knocking over her stool. "Awake."

"He's hungry, Mama."

Brandr swallowed, and his throat clicked. He didn't feel like eating, but he was as parched as winter tundra.

The little girl started toward him with her bowl, but her mother hauled her back.

"Listen to me," she said sternly. "He is *not* your da. He's a bad man, a *very* bad man. Promise me you won't go near him."

"But—"

"Promise me, Kimbery."

Kimbery sighed unhappily and put her bowl back on the table. "I promise."

A very bad man. Brandr supposed he was that. After all, a good man would never have deserted his wife and children to go a-Viking.

Avril righted her overturned stool. Then she picked up Kimbery and sat her atop it. "You stay here."

She straightened and took a steadying breath. The Northman looked much more menacing now that he was awake. She'd already decided he was astonishingly handsome, but his fierce frown made him look dangerous as well. She glanced at the hound collar and leash, hoping they'd hold. She'd managed to keep their great wolfhound, Finn, at heel on that leash until he'd died last year. But the man probably outweighed the hound three times over. And she'd seen, once she removed his cloak, that he was all muscle and bone. She shivered at the thought of all that male strength.

Still, if her father had taught her one thing, it was never to show fear to the enemy. So she raised her chin and confronted him with a stern scowl. "You. Can you understand me?"

He glowered at her through the strands of his hair, but didn't reply.

"Your ship." She pounded one fist into her palm, then exploded her fingers outward to indicate a crash. "How many men were on board?"

He continued to glare at her.

She counted on her fingers. "How many?"

He could understand her. She knew he could. Hell, even Kimbery could understand what she was asking. But he stubbornly refused to answer.

She narrowed her eyes at him. "Damned Viking," she sneered, biting out a word he'd surely recognize.

His lip curled slowly into a grim smile.

An uneasy tremor slithered up her spine, but she refused to let him frighten her. The man was chained to the wall, after all. She had the upper hand. He was at her mercy. She was in control. She'd been trained for command, and she knew how to wield it. If only he wouldn't stare at her with those piercing blue eyes.

She picked up the fireplace poker. It felt good in her grip, like a weapon. "I know your kind," she told him, smacking the poker against her palm in threat. "You're not the first Viking I've met."

His gaze slipped to Kimbery, as if he understood her perfectly and had divined her entire sordid history. Avril's nostrils flared, and her cheeks grew hot. She leaned forward out of Kimbery's hearing to snarl under her breath. "That's right. After slaughtering half my people—men, women, and children—one of your kind took me by force and left me with a babe." She licked her lip, inventing a more satisfactory end to the story. "When I was through with him, he was unable to breed again."

A long silence followed as he stared at her, his face expressionless. She decided he must not be able to understand her after all.

She backed away, turning to jab at the coals on the hearth. "How unlucky for you, Viking," she said with a

self-satisfied smirk. "You come to invade my land and end up shipwrecked on my beach. Maybe that will teach you savages to stay where you belong."

Brandr creased his brow. Where he belonged. He didn't belong anywhere. He had no home, not anymore. The place he'd once called home was full of painful memories, and he had no wish to return there.

Had he come to invade her land? Aye. Had he meant to plunder it? Absolutely. But he'd come to settle here, not to wage war. He only meant to kill if he had to. He wasn't a savage. Of course he'd taken slaves before. But none of his men brandished their weapons without good cause. And none would ever bed a woman against her will.

The Vikings who'd come before must have been berserkers. Such men ingested peculiar mushrooms that made them crazed and violent, driven to mow down everything in their path. To Brandr, they were worse than wild animals.

"I expect your shipmates will be washing ashore soon," the woman mused, replacing the poker. She gazed into the fire, adding sardonically, "I hope I have enough leashes."

Brandr tightened his jaw. He doubted any of his shipmates were alive. No one should have survived that storm. The fact that he'd been spared was proof that Loki, that mischief-making god, wasn't finished torturing him.

He didn't know what had happened to his brothers' ships. The tempest had roared to life halfway through the voyage, and the three vessels had become quickly separated. Even if Halfdan and Ragnarr somehow miraculously managed to sail into the storm and come out the other side, it was unlikely they'd end up on the same stretch of the winding Pictish coast.

"Meanwhile," the woman considered, "what do I do with you?"

She gave him a thorough perusal that ordinarily would have been flattering. But where most women gazed at Brandr as if imagining exactly what they wanted to do with him, she looked as if she hadn't the slightest idea.

"I could turn you over to the lawmen," she murmured. "If you're lucky, they'll hang you quick."

He doubted that. If berserkers had wreaked havoc here, the villagers would more likely stand in line to exact revenge on a Viking trussed up for their pleasure. They'd delight in tearing him to pieces.

"I can't keep you here," she said to herself.

She was right about that, he thought, staring straight ahead, betraying no emotion. She damned well *couldn't* keep him here. He'd allow no one to keep him on a leash, least of all a puny Pictish lass.

The woman continued to contemplate his fate aloud while, behind her, her daughter quietly inched her stool forward.

"The last thing I need," the woman said, "is a third mouth to feed."

A third. So she lived alone here with her daughter. His gaze went to the sword propped in the corner. Then whose was that? Maybe, he thought morosely, it had belonged to the *last* man she'd tied up in her cottage.

The little girl picked up the stool beneath her, toddled a few steps closer, and sat back down.

The woman sighed peevishly. "I should have tossed you back into the sea while I had the chance."

The little girl stared intently at Brandr as she tiptoed forward again with the stool.

"It would probably be a kindness to kill you," the woman muttered, "before someone with less mercy finds you here."

The little girl took two more cautious steps forward and sat down an arm's-length behind her mother, watching him fearlessly.

"And it'd be no less than you deser—" She whirled and almost tripped over the little girl. "Kimbery!" She glanced back at him, blushing, then turned to confront her wayward daughter. "I told you to stay."

"I did stay. See?" She pointed to the stool beneath her, blinking in all innocence.

The woman growled in frustration. Then a strange thing happened. The little girl flashed Brandr a conspiratorial grin, and, of their own accord, his lips curved slightly in answer. It was his first genuine smile in almost a year.

"Mama," Kimbery said sweetly, "I don't want my pottage. You can give it to my da."

The woman spoke between clenched teeth. "Once and for all, Kimbery, he is *not*—"

"Your mother's right," Brandr interjected. "I'm not your da. I'm a bad man, a *very* bad man, and you should stay away."

Avril's jaw dropped. Damn the Viking! He did speak her language, which meant he could understand her perfectly well. "You!" she spat in annoyance, at a loss for words. "You...stop speaking to my daughter."

He did. But his compliance didn't keep her from feeling suddenly threatened. She didn't know why. After all, he was bound, injured, and at her mercy. Still, that he'd been able to deceive her troubled her greatly. And the fact he was warning Kimbery away didn't fit with her assessment of him as a depraved killer. His manner— part devious, part disarming—was definitely unnerving. And she hated to be unnerved.

"Kimmie," she said over her shoulder, "go to bed."

"But I'm not sleepy."

"Go to bed. Now."

Kimbery stuck out her bottom lip, and then flounced off the stool and stomped off, whimpering under her breath.

Avril took a moment to compose herself, and then turned to him, crossing her arms over her chest. "I want some answers, and I want them—"

"Twenty."

"What?"

"Twenty." At her furrowed brow, he added, "You asked how many men were aboard my ship."

She swallowed hard. The berserkers had had at least twice that number. Still, twenty was nineteen more men than she could handle at the moment.

"Where were you headed?"

He shrugged.

"You don't know?" That she didn't believe. The Northmen were notoriously good navigators.

"I didn't care."

His words chilled her. But she supposed she should have expected as much. Barbarians like him scoured the seas, wreaking havoc wherever they landed, unmindful of the devastation they left behind, the people they killed, the lives they destroyed.

"I'd wager you care now," she said with grim threat. "You made a grave error, Viking, landing on my shore."

The doubtful arch of his brow was admittedly subtle. But Avril recognized scorn when she saw it. Men had always questioned her strength, her judgment, and her skill with a blade. At one time, it had infuriated her. Five years ago, she might have succumbed to the impulse to draw her sword to show him just how capable she was.

But she'd learned to rein in her temper. The last time she'd drawn a blade impulsively, she'd wound up at the mercy of a berserker. She wouldn't let it happen again. Besides, what satisfaction could be derived from turning a sword on a helpless captive?

He was staring at her again with his penetrating eyes. She didn't think she'd ever seen eyes so blue—as blue as a summer sky, nay, a robin's egg. Rattled, she turned aside to add another log to the fire.

"I think your arm is broken," she mumbled. Why she'd told him that, she didn't know. After all, it didn't matter. She wasn't about to fix it for him.

"It's a wonder my head isn't broken," he said with a humorless smirk.

She blushed at the reminder of her unchivalrous blow and picked up the poker again, eager to change the subject. "How is it you know my language?"

"I learned it from a Pict slave."

She clenched her teeth. A slave? She jabbed at the glowing coals, but refused to rise to the bait. Maybe she should turn *him* into a slave.

As if he'd read her mind, he asked, "What do you intend to do with me?"

She'd been asking herself that same question all morning. For the moment, she'd hold him hostage. If any of his men turned up alive, she might be able to bargain for her safety with his life. But she wasn't sure there were survivors. Even if there were, there was no telling whether he was of any value to them. The Northmen didn't seem to have the same regard for life as her people did.

"I haven't decided yet," she said.

"If you're going to kill me," he growled, "get it over with."

She frowned. Kill him? In cold blood? Obviously, he knew nothing about chivalry. She straightened with pride, planting the poker between her feet like a blade. "I can't do that. Unlike you, my sense of honor prevents me from slaying unarmed men."

He lifted a brow in mockery. "Give me a blade then," he suggested.

Avril gave him a sardonic smirk. She wasn't so foolhardy as to think she could easily triumph over a gargantuan Northman. But she didn't appreciate his insulting attitude. "I may be honorable, but I'm not soft in the head."

He half-smiled. "You look soft to me."

Her composure slipped, but only for an instant. "I assure you, you wouldn't be the first man I sent limping from the field of battle."

His eyes narrowed suggestively. "And you wouldn't be the first woman I laid out flat on her back."

CHAPTER 3

Brandr regretted his words as soon as he spoke them. He'd forgotten she'd been the victim of rape.

She winced as if he'd struck her, and then recovered so quickly he thought he'd imagined her hurt. "No doubt," she coldly replied.

For some absurd reason, he suddenly wanted to defend himself. He wanted to tell her that he wasn't a berserker. He'd never killed a man without just cause. And he'd never forced himself upon a woman. True, he'd bedded more than his share of eager wenches in his youth, but only at their invitation. And once he'd taken a wife...

Then he gave his head a mental shake. What was he thinking? It didn't matter what the woman thought of him. They were foes. She probably intended to kill him anyway. If she'd been exposed to berserkers from the North—the kind that violated women, murdered priests,

and slaughtered children—she had every cause to want him dead.

And yet there were qualities about her—her independence, her intelligence, her patience with her daughter, the way she talked about honor—that told him she might not kill him needlessly. She might listen to reason.

That was why he'd volunteered the truth about his men and his ship. His fate rested in her hands at the moment. If he gave her cause for mistrust, she wouldn't hesitate to slay him. He'd do the same in her position.

But if he endeared himself to her, if he made her look at him, not as a Viking, but as a man, she'd have a harder time killing him...and maybe he'd buy himself time to overpower her and escape.

"You know, I'm not really the savage you think I am," he confided.

She ignored him, setting aside the poker and going into the kitchen.

"I had a family," he called after her, "a daughter like yours." He silently cursed as his voice caught on the words.

She froze for a moment, and then cleared her empty shell bowl from the table.

He added, "I, too, would have protected her from men like me."

She paused again, then sighed and picked up the little girl's half-eaten pottage. "It's cold," she grumbled, approaching to give him the bowl, "but it'll fill your belly."

Pain seared his cracked forearm as he lifted the bowl

with his bound hands to tip the contents into his mouth. But it was better than starving to death. He finished the pottage in three gulps, and then lowered his hands to rest them limply on his lap, letting the bowl slip through his fingers and onto the floor.

The woman returned to her fire-tending. Her face glowed golden as she gazed into the flames, and her hair shone with reflected firelight. "You said you *had* a daughter." She asked casually, "What happened to her?"

It had been almost a year, but the wound still felt new and raw. "She died," he said flatly. Just speaking the words aloud hurt.

The air grew still. For a long while, she didn't speak.

Finally she asked, "How?"

He swallowed down the knot of pain in his throat. He didn't want to talk about it. He didn't know this woman. She was his enemy. Why should he tell her anything? And yet something compelled him to speak. Maybe it was the soft encouragement in her voice. Maybe it was the dewy compassion in her eyes. Maybe it was the fact that he had nothing more to lose. "Plague."

Her forehead creased, and she propped the poker against the hearth. "And her mother?"

His cruel mind conjured up Inga's precious face. "Dead," he told her woodenly. "My daughter. My wife. My son. All dead."

He heard the woman's soft gasp, but she had no words of comfort for him. There weren't any. There was nothing anyone could say to bring back his family.

After a bit, she murmured, "But you survived."

"Oh, aye." Bitter regret twisted his mouth as he sneered, "I was lucky. I was at sea."

The woman's brow furrowed. She leaned forward almost imperceptibly. For a curious instant, as she looked at him with liquid brown eyes full of empathy, he imagined she meant to touch his hand in solace.

But he'd never be sure, because at that moment, the little girl peered around the doorway. "Mama," she sang out cheerfully, "I'm finished sleeping."

"Kimbery!" the woman cried, coloring and rising briskly.

Avril felt the way she had when her father had caught her kissing the stable boy. Which was ridiculous. After all, she'd done nothing to be ashamed of. But a strange guilt lingered in the air. She'd almost reached out to comfort the Northman. And she didn't know why.

Flustered, she scooped up the empty bowl and turned to face Kimbery.

"I'm all better now, Mama," the wee lass said, using her sweetest, most cunning voice.

Avril sighed and shook her head, then carried the bowl into the kitchen.

Kimbery's wiles left Avril with a dilemma. Avril needed to search the beach to see if any more Northmen had made landfall. But it was too risky taking Kimbery with her. If there were shipwreck survivors, she didn't want to put her daughter in harm's way. And if there weren't, she didn't need her little girl seeing a dozen half-eaten corpses washing up on her shore.

She needed Kimbery to stay in the cottage. But she didn't trust the wee lass with the man she kept insisting

was her da. He might very well talk her into setting him free.

She had a choice then. She could either tie up her daughter, or she could drug the Northman.

The decision took an instant.

"You must be thirsty," she called to him.

She needn't have worried he'd taste the opium powder she put in his mead. He gulped it down eagerly and wanted more. While she kept Kimbery occupied churning sheep's milk into butter, he began to get drowsy. By the time his suspicions were aroused, it was too late.

"What'd y' put...in th' drink?" he asked, slurring the words.

"Nothing poisonous," she told him. "Don't fret. You'll just sleep for a while."

With his last bit of strength, he growled at her in impotent anger, and then he slumped against the beam.

"G'night, Da," Kimbery called merrily as she plunged the dasher up and down in the wooden churn.

Avril swirled her cloak over her shoulders. "Kimmie, I'm going down to the beach. I need you to stay here and keep churning."

She nodded.

"Stay away from the man. I'll be back soon."

"Shh," she whispered. "Da's sleeping. Don't wake him up."

Avril glanced at the softly snoring Viking, who looked far less threatening in slumber. His scowl was gone. His muscles were lax. His mouth fell open like Kimbery's when she was sleeping. With his broad shoulders, his strong jaw, and his breathtaking eyes, he was truly one of the most attractive men she'd ever seen. Indeed, she could almost imagine him, not as a treacherous Northman, but as a little girl's father. Almost.

On her way to the beach, Avril grabbed the sharpened spade from the garden. It would serve to either bury the dead or defend her from the living.

It was midday by the time she returned to the cottage. She'd found no bodies or evidence of survivors, just a few splintered planks from his longship. A lot of driftwood, however, had washed ashore from the tempest, enough to keep their hearth burning all winter. It would take more than one trip to bring it all home.

To her surprise, when she dropped her first burden at the threshold and pushed open the door to check on Kimbery, the little girl was still sitting dutifully at her post, churning butter. But then Avril glanced over at the snoring Northman. Kimbery's stuffed cloth doll was tucked into the crook of his arm.

"Kimbery," she chided.

"He was lonely," the little girl explained.

Avril shook her head. Kimbery was probably right. The man had lost his shipmates, his wife, and his children. She couldn't imagine how awful that must be. If she lost Kimbery...

It was too awful to contemplate. Her daughter was all she had now.

She took the lid off the churn to show Kimbery how all her hard work had magically separated the cream. She poured the buttermilk off into a small cask and wrapped the lump of butter into a piece of dried kelp.

But then she needed to think up a new task to keep Kimbery occupied while she collected the rest of her scavenge. She plucked a small piece of cool charcoal from the fire and gave it to the little girl, along with the pale, flat slate they used for writing.

"Why don't you practice your letters?" she suggested. Avril's father had insisted Avril learn to read so she'd be better able to manage Rivenloch. Avril was determined to pass the skill on to her daughter.

Kimbery picked up the charcoal and, pressing her lips together in concentration, drew a straight vertical line.

"I'm going out again," Avril told her. "I'll see what you've written when I come back."

It took three more treks to collect the store of driftwood. Satisfied with her haul, which she stacked beside the cottage, she dusted off her skirts and opened the door.

"Look, Mama!" Kimbery squealed, hopping down from her stool. "Look what I made!"

Avril studied the slate. Kimbery had printed the letters D and A, and beneath was a primitive sketch of their prisoner, bound with rope, with her doll nestled in one arm.

Avril wanted to be perturbed, but it was admittedly a decent drawing for a four-year-old. "That's very good, Kimmie. Now why don't you draw a picture of a starfish?"

"Nay!" she said, covering the slate with her arms to keep Avril from wiping it clean. "I want to show him."

"But he's sleeping."

"He'll wake up."

Avril wondered. She hadn't put that much powder in his drink—certainly not much more than she did on occasions when her monthly courses became unbearable—but opium could be risky.

His arm looked awful. It was still swollen, and the skin of his forearm had a bluish cast. If he'd been someone she cared about, she would have set it and made him a splint so it would heal straight. But it seemed like a waste of time and effort when she wasn't even sure she was going to let him live, let alone recover from his injuries.

As it turned out, he slept through Kimbery's afternoon nap and their abalone supper. When Kimbery crept into bed with a huge yawn, he was still sleeping. And he hadn't awakened when Avril blew out the candles and made her way to bed.

But in the middle of the night, she was roused by the sound of scuffling in the next room, and she crept out to investigate, a dagger in her hand.

By the dim light of the banked fire, she saw the Northman beginning to wake. His movements were sluggish, and his eyelids flagged as he struggled to sit upright.

She moved forward to get a closer look, hunkering down beside him.

When his gaze alit on her, a look of wonder came over

36

his face. His eyes lit up with pleasure and relief. "Inga," he breathed.

She frowned and opened her mouth, intending to correct him. But when she saw the affection in his eyes, she found she didn't have the heart.

"Inga." He smiled, his eyes twinkling.

She gulped, reluctant to break the fragile thread of his happy delusion.

He reached up with his bound hands and took her chin in gentle fingers. Before she realized what he was doing, he tilted his head and captured her lips with his.

For an instant she froze, stunned. Swiftly, the softness of his mouth, the warmth of his touch, the sweetness of his kiss enthralled her, and she melted into his welcoming embrace. He tasted of the sea and adventure and passion. And for one sliver of a moment in time, it was possible to believe he had feelings for her.

Then she remembered who he was and that he'd called her by another woman's name.

With a soft cry of resistance, she tore free, covering her mutinous mouth with the back of one trembling hand and holding her dagger out before her.

Oblivious to her blade, he mumbled something in his own tongue then and, with a peaceful sigh, slumped back into slumber.

Avril scrambled back, scrubbing at her lips. God's eyes! How could she have let him kiss her? He was a Northman—a savage, a barbarian, a dog. His kind were rapists and plunderers. Shite, she should have killed him while she had the chance.

Yet even though she steeled her heart against him, his taste lingered on her lips, taunting her. Returning to bed, she found it impossible to get back to sleep as unsavory memories rose to the surface of her thoughts.

It had been a long time since she'd been kissed by a man. And she'd never been kissed so tenderly.

Though she'd tried to deny it, rape had left her damaged. The loss of power, the helplessness had cut her deeply. For a long while afterwards, she hadn't been able to endure a man's glance, much less his touch. She'd wanted to crawl away in defeat, to hide in shame and lick her wounds.

But she knew that would have meant her rapist had won and that she'd bear those scars the rest of her life. So instead, she'd decided to deal with the trauma the same way she handled falling off a horse or being knocked down in a swordfight.

She'd faced her fears, diving headfirst back into the fray. Though she wasn't particularly proud of her rash behavior now, she'd begun bedding men indiscriminately, forcing them to submit to her will, enjoying a heady triumph when they surrendered beneath her. Eventually, she'd overcome her feelings of powerlessness and vulnerability.

It appalled her now to think of the men she'd seduced and cast away. On the other hand, when she'd finally realized that she was pregnant, not one of them had come forward to claim the babe and salvage her honor.

Of course, after she gave birth to a fair-haired girl who was obviously the offspring of a Viking, she was shunned by all. She'd had to face the hard truth—she'd never find a man willing to play father to a Viking's child and husband to a woman stripped of her title, her land, and her wealth.

She'd shut off that part of her that longed for family, friends, and love, hidden it away behind the locked door to her heart.

But that kiss...that kiss had turned the key in the door and stirred feelings in her she'd forgotten—feelings of tenderness, affection, and hope. And it was a long while before her restless emotions let her drift off to sleep.

Brandr wandered all night in the land between waking and sleeping. He wasn't sure what was real and what he dreamed. But now morning had arrived, and his body couldn't have felt more substantial to him. His tongue was stuck to the roof of his mouth. His eyes were gummed shut. His hands were numb.

She'd drugged him. He remembered that much. The mead she'd given him had been laced with something that had sent him into a hallucination-riddled oblivion.

If only it had left him there...

Sensing someone near, he cracked open one eyelid. In the dim light, he could see the little blonde girl crouched beside him with an empty chamberpot, studying his face.

"Kimmie!" her mother shouted, startling the child. "Get away from him!"

The little girl did as she was told, dropping the chamberpot beside him with a loud clank. Then she crossed her arms importantly over her chest and said something she'd probably heard before from her mother. "If you can't take good care of your pets, you can't keep them."

"He's not a—," she said, snagging the little girl's hand to drag her back. "I told you, Kimmie, he's a bad man."

Brandr opened both eyes now. Even mussed from slumber, the woman was lovely. Tendrils of hair had pulled loose from her braid and framed her face like seaweed draped artfully on a sandy shore. Beneath her kirtle, her rumpled white underdress was untied at the throat, revealing the subtle curve of her bosom. And her sleep-swollen lips…

He frowned. A strange memory tugged at his brain. Had he…kissed the woman?

Her fleeting glance and the guilt in her eyes confirmed his suspicion. He *had* kissed her. But when? And why?

Her gaze drifted and settled upon his lap, and suddenly he wondered if he'd done more than just kiss her. Had he taken liberties with her that he couldn't recall?

"Kimbery," she said, continuing to stare with discomfiting boldness, "bring Mama her dagger."

His breath caught. Her dagger? What did she mean to do? Surely she wouldn't…cut anything off of him in front of her daughter. Would she? He tried to ask her what she intended, but his mouth was too dry to speak.

Once she had the dagger in her hand, she approached him, and he drew his legs back defensively.

"Listen," she confided softly so her daughter wouldn't

hear. "I'm going to cut your wrists free. But if you try anything, I swear I'll plunge this dagger into your throat."

He looked down at his hands, resting on his lap. No wonder he couldn't feel them. The ropes were cutting into his swollen wrists, and the fingers of his left hand were blue.

"Do you understand?" she said, narrowing flinty eyes at him.

He nodded.

She sliced him free, and he bit back a groan of pain as sensation suddenly stabbed into his fingers like a thousand agonizing needles. He felt the blood drain from his face as he fought to stay conscious.

"Kimmie, bring me a cup of water, please."

The little girl hurried to comply. Why the woman was showing him mercy, he didn't know. Perhaps it was only that she didn't want his death on her conscience. But he gladly accepted the water as she tipped the cup back for him, coughing as he drank too swiftly.

Whether she would have actually slit his throat in front of the little girl, he didn't know, but he wasn't about to put her to the test.

"Kimbery," she called over her shoulder, her blade resting against his neck. "I need you to wait in bed until I call you."

"But, Mama, I want to help, too."

"Not yet. In a moment."

Brandr didn't like the sound of that. What did the woman want to do that she didn't want her daughter to see?

"Promise?" the little girl asked.

"I promise. Now wait there till I call you."

The lass skipped off, and Brandr was left alone with the woman.

She stared at her blade where it contacted his throat, muttering irritably to herself. "I should just let you go on suffering. God knows you would have shown me no mercy." She glanced down at his misshapen arm. "If I do this for you," she said, sighing, "if I put you out of your misery—"

By Odin, she meant to kill him! His warrior instincts took over, and despite her menacing blade, despite the wrenching pain in his arms, with the last of his strength, he reached up with his good hand and roughly seized her wrist, giving it a sharp flick and sending the dagger clattering across the floor.

For an instant, their eyes met, and he saw true panic there as he gained the upper hand. But his advantage was short-lived. In the next breath, she drove her free fist forward and punched him hard in the nose.

CHAPTER 4

The Viking instantly lost his grip on her, and Avril tumbled back onto her hindquarters, cradling her bruised knuckles. What was wrong with the man? Hadn't she said she was going to put him out of his misery? The ungrateful wretch!

He was subdued now, and blood dripped from one nostril. She hadn't hit him hard enough to break his nose. Indeed, she hadn't knocked him out, only stunned him. She'd have to work quickly before he took it into his head to fight off her good intentions again.

She carefully moved his injured arm flat on his lap and pushed up his sleeve to examine it. The bone looked fairly straight, though it was hard to tell from the swelling. She ran her fingertips gently and swiftly along the edges of his forearm to check for breaks.

Nothing poked through the flesh, so it wasn't too serious. But halfway between his elbow and his wrist, there was a bulge where the bone had cracked and slipped sideways. She'd have to pull it and put it back into alignment.

Why she was showing him any kindness, she didn't know. Maybe it was because he'd lost his wife and children. Maybe it was because he was alone, abandoned, a castaway like her. Maybe it was the way he'd kissed her last night.

He was coming around again, sniffing back the blood trickling from his nose. She'd have to move fast. Seizing his thick wrist in both her hands, she thrust her foot against the inside of his elbow and pulled hard.

He bellowed, but he must have understood what she was doing. His right hand was free, and he could have flattened her with one punch. Instead, he pounded the floor with his fist.

She let go of him then and backed away. She wasn't sure what black words he spat out, for they were in his own tongue. But the rafters rang with his curses, and Kimbery couldn't resist the urge to peek around the corner at the great roaring beast.

"Mama, what are you—"

"Go!" they shouted simultaneously, and Kimbery disappeared at once.

The Northman was huffing like a wounded wolf now, and she realized he was just as dangerous. She'd set his arm. And now he might well be able to use it.

She armed herself with the fireplace poker, ready to jab him at a moment's notice. But he didn't seem inclined to aggression. His legs were bound. His upper arms were secure. The leash was still in place. He couldn't go anywhere.

"The break should heal properly now, but you'll need a splint. Move," she said, showing him the poker, "and I'll break your other arm."

Luckily she had a choice selection of driftwood just outside. Leaving the door open, she ducked out, quickly chose two fairly straight sticks, and brought them in, thinking all the while she must be mad. Mending a Viking invader made as much sense as sewing up a deer she'd shot for supper.

She rummaged in the small chest at the hearth and found a linen underdress that had grown too small for Kimbery. She ripped it into strips to use for binding. "Do I need to give you opium again to keep you calm?"

"Nay," he growled.

She still didn't trust him. "Then heed me well, Northman. Make one false move, and I'll unset your arm again as fast as I set it."

He let her splint his arm, but it proved almost as much an ordeal for her as it was for him. It felt wrong, touching him. His arm looked foreign and forbidding with its massive muscle and sprinkling of light golden hair. His tawny skin was hot beneath her fingers, as if it radiated sunlight, and her own flesh grew warm from the contact. She was close enough to feel his breath, and her pulse quickened as she remembered the pleasant sensation of his lips on hers. The kiss had been so unexpectedly gentle coming from a brutal Northman.

But she couldn't afford to be gulled by his tenderness. Besides, he looked anything but tender today. An angry furrow lodged between his brows. The corners of his mouth turned down. And his hands looked enormous and threatening beside hers. A man like him could grasp her neck in one fist and squeeze the life out of her before she could blink.

Fortunately, he didn't.

She managed to tie off the splint and then bound his wrists together again with rope. Satisfied with her work, she backed away, eager to create some distance between her and the man who was disrupting her heartbeat.

Keeping her hands occupied was easy. There were always plenty of chores to be done. She'd gathered seaweed yesterday to make a soup, and now she stood at the table with her wooden block, chopping the ruffled red strands into small pieces. Keeping her mind occupied, however, was almost impossible, especially when she felt the Viking's silent gaze on her like the intent stare of a stalking wolf.

After several unnerving moments, he finally spoke. "No chains can hold me forever, woman."

She continued chopping. She worried he was right, but she certainly wasn't about to let him know that.

He continued, "Have you not heard the story of Fenrir?"

She gave him a disinterested sniff.

Which he ignored. "Fenrir, the fearsome son of Loki. They tried to keep *him* chained. Shall I tell you what happened?"

She refused to look at him. "Nay. I have no wish to hear—"

"Tell me! Tell me!" Kimmie suddenly cried from the doorway. "I want to hear a story!"

"Hush!" Avril hissed. "I don't want you going anywhere near him, Kimbery."

"I won't go near him, Mama. I promise. Please?"

"Nay. I don't even want him speaking to you."

"But why?" she whined.

He answered before she could open her mouth. "Your mother is afraid I may turn you into a Viking."

"Oh," Kimmie said.

Avril let out an exasperated breath, slammed down her knife, and glowered at him. "That's not true."

"But Mama, I'm already *half* Viking," she said happily, skipping over to Avril.

Avril bit the inside of her cheek. She usually tried to forget about that half. Despite Kimbery's ice blonde hair and periwinkle blue eyes, she thought of her daughter as a sweet little Pict lass.

"Please, Mama," she wheedled, tugging on Avril's skirts, "I'll be good, I promise."

"*You'll* be good," Avril said, picking up her knife and pointing it toward the Northman. "*He,* however, is not so well-behaved."

"What do you expect I'll do?" he muttered, pointedly twisting his neck in the collar, "Pierce her with my gaze?"

Avril thought he was doing a fairly good job of that already. She felt the touch of his frosty glare like the stabbing of winter sleet.

But he was right. For all intents and purposes, he was helpless. He couldn't harm Kimbery with mere words. Besides, it *would* be useful to have the wee lass entertained while Avril tended to her chores. She'd heard Viking sagas were notoriously lengthy and convoluted, which would keep Kimmie out from under her feet for a while.

Still, she couldn't allow the Northman anywhere near her daughter. He might not be able to escape, but he could do serious damage to a little girl who wandered too close.

"I won't hurt her," he said. "I swear."

Surely he didn't expect her to trust him. A Viking's oath wasn't worth shite. "That's right. You won't. Because if you lay a finger on her, I'll carve you up with this knife."

"Please, Mama?" Kimbery pursed her lips.

Avril sighed. She shook her head, still not sure it was a good idea. "You swear on your honor, Kimbery, that you'll stay where I put you?"

"On my honor," she said, clapping a hand to her chest.

Avril put down her knife and wiped her palms on her apron. She took Kimmie by the hand and walked her to a spot near the hearth, opposite the Viking. "Stay here. And you," she said, stabbing a finger toward her captive. "Don't even cast your 'piercing gaze' on my daughter or I'll gouge out your eyes."

She didn't need to tell him that. He wasn't going to look at her precious Kimbery. His piercing gaze was reserved for the cursed wench who'd clubbed him on the head, dragged him up the beach, tethered him like a rogue hound, and punched him in the nose. He might be telling the tale of Fenrir to her daughter, but his glare and the story were meant for *her*.

"Long ago," he began, staring intently at the woman's back while she chopped seaweed, "Fenrir, one of Loki's three sons—"

"Who's Loki?" Kimmie asked.

"Loki is the brother of Thor."

"Who's Thor?"

"Thor is the son of Odin."

"Who's Odin?"

Brandr sighed. The little girl apparently knew nothing about her Viking bloodline and history. It was tempting to recite the entire lineage of the gods, an ordeal that could take hours, but his own children had always fallen asleep before he could get past the fifth generation. He settled for telling her, "Odin is a god. They're all gods. And Loki, the son of Odin and the god of fire, was always causing trouble."

"Mama says I'm always causing trouble," Kimbery told him.

"Well, not *this* kind of trouble," he said. "Loki lied and cheated and tricked the other gods."

"He had no honor?"

"Aye, that's right. He had no honor. He did, however, have three sons, creatures he'd raised up to be terrible monsters. One was a great serpent." Brandr hissed like a snake, making the little girl shiver in delighted revulsion. The woman ignored his antics.

"Odin cast him into the sea, where he grew so fast that his body coiled around the whole world and his tail grew into his mouth."

The little girl gasped with wonder. Her mother continued chopping.

"The second monster Odin imprisoned in Niflheim, a land where the sun never shines and it's always dark."

"I'm not afraid of the dark," Kimbery boasted.

"That's good."

"What about the third monster?"

"He was called Fenrir, and he was a vicious, snapping wolf." Brandr snarled loudly, startling the woman. She gasped and fumbled with her knife, dropping it with a clatter on the table. He smirked, enormously satisfied. "Odin brought him to Asgard, the home of the gods, hoping to tame him."

"Tame him like Finn?"

"Finn?"

"My dog. He used to let me ride on his back."

"I see. Nay, Fenrir was too wild to be tamed. Each day, he grew bigger and bigger, more and more ferocious, until only one of the gods had the courage to feed him. That god was Tyr, the god of war, another of Odin's sons. Tyr was brave and loyal, and every day he'd bring Fenrir his supper."

"What did Fenrir eat?"

Glancing at the woman, who had gone back to chopping, he was tempted to say "Pictish wenches." Instead, he told her, "He ate meat—cows and pigs and—"

"Sheep?" the lass asked fearfully. "Did he eat sheep? I have a sheep."

"Well...nay, I don't think Fenrir liked the taste of sheep," he assured her. "But he had a big appetite, and he grew larger every day until eventually the gods decided he was too big and too dangerous to be roaming around Asgard. They couldn't kill him, because killing was forbidden in Asgard. So they decided to chain him."

"Like Mama chained you?"

He smiled grimly. "Exactly."

The woman stiffened and paused, her knife poised in midair.

He resumed the story. "Thor, the god of thunder and Loki's brother, said he would forge a strong chain to bind Fenrir with the help of Miolnir."

"Who's Miolnir?"

"Miolnir is Thor's mighty hammer. It looks like the one I wear around my neck." He lifted his chin to show the little girl the small silver hammer.

Kimbery rose up halfway, as if she planned to walk over to get a closer look.

Like all mothers, the woman apparently had eyes in the back of her head, for she called over her shoulder, "Kimmie, stay where you are!"

"I am!" the little girl insisted, sitting back down.

Brandr continued. "Thor hammered all night on the chain. The next day, because Fenrir wasn't afraid of the other gods," he said, narrowing his eyes pointedly at the woman's back, "he let them slip the chain around his neck."

"And nobody was allowed to go near him," Kimbery guessed.

"That's right. But much to the surprise of the gods, Fenrir made one powerful lunge, broke the chain, and freed himself."

The little girl gasped in dismay.

The woman, still with her back turned, interrupted the story. "Well, they obviously didn't use a strong enough chain," she muttered, resuming her chopping.

"Then what happened?" Kimbery asked.

He smiled slyly. "The gods decided they needed a stronger chain." He saw the woman's shoulders rise and fall with an irritated sigh. "So Thor promised he'd work harder this time and make a chain that could never be broken. He hammered at his forge for three days and three nights. When he was done, the chain was so heavy that even mighty Thor could hardly lift it. This time, Fenrir was not so willing to be bound. But the gods praised his great strength and assured Fenrir he could easily break that chain as well. So he finally let them put the chain about his neck."

"Did he break it, too?"

"He gave a great shake of his head," he said, demonstrating, "and a forceful bound, and he broke free of even that chain."

The woman stabbed her knife into the block with a loud clunk, clearly displeased with the direction the story was taking. But he didn't care. He had a point to make. No Pictish woman was going to get the best of him, trying to keep him leashed like Fenrir.

"Then what happened?" Kimbery asked.

"Thor was very discouraged, and the gods didn't know what to do. Finally, Frey, the god of summer, said he would ask the dwarves who lived deep in the earth to forge a chain, for though they were small, they possessed powerful magic. Surely they could make a chain strong enough to hold Fenrir."

The little girl was enthralled now. She sat with her chin in her hands, leaning forward as far as possible. Her mother had begun chopping another batch of seaweed, but he noticed she was doing so quietly. No doubt she was hanging on his every word as well.

"It took them two days and two nights, but the dwarves fashioned a chain out of the six strongest elements they could find. They used the roots of rocks, the spit of birds, the footsteps of cats, the beards of women, the breath of fish, and the sinew of bears. They presented the chain to the gods, and though it was fine and light, the dwarves assured them the magic chain was unbreakable. Of course, by this time, the gods knew Fenrir was too clever to allow them to bind him a third time. So they invited him to join them on a voyage to a beautiful island, where they would play games together and demonstrate feats of strength."

"What's an island?"

He frowned. The little girl *lived* on an island. Didn't she know that? "Land surrounded by water."

"Like my house?"

"Aye."

"Nay," the woman countered, "it isn't the same, Kimmie. We only live *beside* the ocean."

"You live on an island," he told her.

"We do not," the woman said, turning to him with a scowl.

"It's a large island, to be sure, but—"

"We don't live on an island."

He arched a brow in challenge. "Really? How do you know? Have *you* ever sailed the seas?"

The woman gave him an affronted sniff and turned back to her work, clearly upset by this revelation.

Avril was positive the Viking was wrong. She'd traveled for days—north, south, and west—and never run into the sea. But the marauders of the North sailed great distances. If anyone knew the oceans, it was a Northman. The idea that she might live on an island was disconcerting. The idea that he knew her home better than she did troubled her greatly.

"Then what happened?" Kimmie asked. "Then what?"

"The gods brought out the chain, and they all tried to break it, but none could do it, not even Thor, who said it was so strong that surely only Fenrir could break it. Fenrir was too proud to refuse their challenge. He allowed them to place the chain around his neck on one condition—that one of the gods put his right hand in Fenrir's mouth while they did so as an act of faith, to prove they didn't mean to imprison him."

Kimbery gasped.

"The gods, of course, *did* mean to imprison him, so no one wanted to put a hand in Fenrir's mouth. But loyal Tyr stepped bravely forward and placed his hand between the wolf's sharp teeth. They put the chain around Fenrir's neck, and Fenrir tried to break it, but the more he lunged, the tighter the chain became. When he found he couldn't get free, he snapped his jaws in anger and bit off Tyr's hand."

"Oh, nay!" Kimbery cried.

Avril turned to address her daughter. "Which is why, Kimmie, we don't go near dangerous chained beasts." She lifted a smug brow at him.

He returned a smug brow and replied, "Which is why we shouldn't keep 'dangerous beasts' chained."

"Did Tyr die?" Kimmie asked.

"Nay, he didn't die," the man said. "He became a hero in Asgard because of his bravery."

"Mama, I want to go to Asgard."

Avril gave the Viking a long-suffering glower. He smiled in return.

"Kimmie," she said, "come help me wash the sloke."

Kimbery skipped over and plopped down on her stool while Avril brought her a bucket of fresh water. The little girl pushed up her sleeves and thrust her arms into the water, stirring vigorously as Avril dumped the chopped seaweed into the bucket.

The Viking's story had been completely absurd, of course. There was no such place as Asgard, no god with a hammer, no dwarves who forged magical chains. Still, the tale had been entertaining enough, and it had kept Kimmie occupied.

The man had been right about one thing, however. Avril did harbor the fear that Kimbery's Viking blood might be stirred to life one day, that she would become enthralled by the mysterious world of her Viking father, and that Avril would somehow lose her Pictish daughter to the marauders of the North.

She could feel the Viking's ice-blue eyes on her as she coaxed the fire to life and added more wood. His attention was quite disturbing. But then there wasn't much else for him to look at, she supposed. She was tempted to blindfold him, but that seemed

unnecessarily cruel. If only he wouldn't watch her every move...

"That's good, Kimmie. We'll put it on to boil now and go milk Caimbeul."

It could do no harm to leave the Viking alone at this point. He seemed adequately trussed up. They'd be gone only a short while, long enough to milk the ewe and turn her into the pasture.

CHAPTER 5

The instant they closed the cottage door, Brandr began struggling at his bonds, praying for Fenrir's strength. The way he saw it, eventually the woman would tire of having him in her cottage. But she wouldn't just set him free. She'd turn him over to someone who knew what to do with a captive Viking. The last thing he wanted was to force her into a hasty decision.

He strained with all his might against the leather collar. With his arm splinted, it was even more useless now. But if he pulled hard enough, he might be able to work the iron ring out of the wall. Once that was done, he could reach the knot to free his ankles. Then he'd flee. And he'd take that magnificent sword with him.

Where he'd go, he didn't know. It wouldn't be easy for a tall, blond, blue-eyed Northman to hide in this land of dark-haired dwarves.

The leather rubbed his throat raw, and he nearly

choked himself more than once, but he couldn't dislodge the ring. When they returned, he was no closer to freedom. The woman, however, suspected something, for she gave him a sharp look as she set a bucket of milk on the table.

"You're sweating," she said.

"I'm beside the fire," he replied.

She frowned dubiously and opened her mouth to speak, but Kimbery interrupted her. "I milked Caimbeul," she announced proudly. "Her name's Caimbeul because she has a crooked mouth, like this." She made a comical sneer. "Have *you* ever milked a sheep?"

He shook his head.

"Indeed?" her mother asked with a sly lift of her brow. "I'll have to teach you how when your arm heals."

He narrowed his eyes. Teach him to milk a sheep? Did she plan to enslave him? The idea was absurd. He was the son of a noble, a warrior. And unless she meant to keep him tied up, he'd easily fight his way free. A featherweight wench and her four-year-old daughter were no match for a Viking.

But this was good news. Without the imminent threat of death and with the benefit of time, he could easily lull her into a false trust. Then, when she least expected it, he'd manage his escape.

"Want to see my picture?" Kimbery asked him. She didn't wait for an answer, galloping into the bedchamber and returning with a square piece of slate.

He turned his head to look at it. "Is that me?"

She nodded.

"Did you draw it?"

She nodded again.

"What does it say?"

"Kimbery," her mother interrupted, "don't bother him."

"I'm not." Then she pointed to the letters, confiding to him in a loud whisper, "It says Da."

He couldn't help but smile at that. The little girl certainly was bullheaded.

Her mother, obviously eager to end their conversation, asked, "How is the sloke doing, Kimmie?"

Kimbery set the slate down and peered into the clay pot nestled amongst the coals. "It's bubbling, Mama."

"Good. Don't stand too close to the fire."

The little girl took a dramatic step backward and started idly twirling her braid between her fingers. Her gaze slid over to him, then to the floor, and she wrinkled her forehead in concern. Following her eyes, he saw he was crushing her cloth doll beneath his hip. He moved aside as much as he could, which wasn't very much.

"Mama," she said plaintively, "I want Maeve back."

The woman clucked her tongue. "You shouldn't have given her to him."

Kimbery's bottom lip trembled.

The woman sighed softly. "Very well. You stay back. I'll get her."

She approached carefully and crouched beside him. She smelled fresh, like sunshine and sweet grass. Her underdress was still untied, and when she bent forward, he could see the upper crescent of her breast, as pale and smooth as cream. A surge of lust rose in him, and it

wasn't helped by the fact that she began rummaging under his buttock for the doll.

His uneasy grunt alerted her to what she was doing. Suddenly mortified, she seized the doll and yanked it out, unfortunately tearing its arm in the process.

Naturally, Kimbery began screaming in horror at the sight, and it took several moments before her mother could placate her with the fact that the doll could be easily repaired.

Meanwhile, Brandr was glad his hands were bound over his lap, for the sight of his rising desire would undoubtedly upset them even more. It certainly upset *him*. He'd lost his wife less than a year ago. It wasn't right that he should be aroused by this strange woman.

Eventually order was restored, though the woman had to pause in her other chores to stitch the doll's arm back on. When she was finished, the little girl studied her handiwork intently to be sure it was correct. Apparently satisfied, she took the doll into her bedchamber, chattering to it all the way.

The woman was busy the rest of the day. He'd never seen anyone work so hard. Even the thralls of his country were allowed to rest. But she labored from sunrise to well after sunset, keeping the fire stoked, preparing supper, milking the sheep, laundering linens, making cheese, mending clothes, even teaching her daughter to read and write. No wonder she wanted to make a slave out of him.

The seaweed pottage was remarkably tasty, especially after she added the fresh sheep's milk, smoked fish, and wild onions to it. It might not be the succulent roast pig he preferred, but he had to admire her ability to make delicious fare out of what was at hand. Indeed, if he'd come to Pictland for pillage and prisoners, he would have considered himself lucky to take such a resourceful woman home as a slave.

At the end of the day, the woman heated water for Kimbery's bath and undressed her. As the little girl streaked through the cottage naked, squealing that she didn't want a bath, Brandr had to bite back a smile. Eventually, her mother caught her and plopped her into a makeshift tub of a split ale cask. After a bit, the little girl's protests subsided, and she began playing in the water, singing and splashing. By the time she was scrubbed clean, her mother's kirtle was drenched, and Kimbery now didn't want to get *out* of the tub.

She kicked and screamed as her mother picked her up. Brandr, amused by the wicked little sprite's antics, couldn't help but laugh aloud.

Avril turned in surprise. The Northman was grinning. His eyes sparkled like the sunlit sea, and his teeth flashed as white as snow. But it was the low rumble of his laughter that took her breath away. She didn't realize how much she'd missed that sound. She hadn't heard male laughter in four long years.

Then Kimbery, wet and slippery, taking advantage of Avril's distraction, slid out of her grasp and began tearing around the cottage. She dodged the linen Avril held out until Avril finally gave up, figuring the little girl would dry herself off with her running.

The Viking's smile turned bittersweet then, and a faraway look came into his eyes. Avril knew at once that he must be remembering his own daughter.

She forced her gaze away, dabbing at her damp kirtle with the linen. It wasn't her concern. His people hadn't cared whose children they slaughtered when they'd raided Rivenloch. Why should she care what had happened to his daughter? And yet, against her will, words fell softly from her lips. "What was your daughter's name?"

He glanced up, as if surprised she'd read his thoughts. "Asta."

"It's a pretty name."

"She was a pretty..." He choked on the words. "A pretty lass."

She shouldn't feel sorry for him. The Vikings killed pretty Pictish lasses all the time. But there was a deep sorrow in the Northman's eyes that pulled at her heart.

"Who's Inga?" The words tumbled out of her mouth unbidden, mortifying her. She should never have asked him that. He probably didn't remember calling her by that name or kissing her anyway.

His gaze shot straight to hers.

"You...spoke her name in your sleep," she explained.

He frowned. "I dreamt she was alive."

"Your wife," she guessed.

He nodded.

He must have loved her well. That kiss had been full of tenderness and desire. As odd as it was, Avril envied the dead woman. His fortunate Inga had known the love of a devoted husband. Avril had only experienced the mindless lust of a Viking berserker and a handful of men for whom she felt nothing.

Just then Kimbery went galloping past. Before Avril could catch her, the wee lass dove at the shocked Northman. She plopped herself into his lap and captured his gold-stubbled face playfully between her hands.

"Da!" she cried.

Avril's heart leaped into her mouth. Tiny, pale, bare Kimbery looked so vulnerable against the Viking's broad chest. Lord, he could bite off her hand with one snap of his jaws, just like that wolf in his story.

She glanced up in horror at his face. But he looked far more rattled than she was. No doubt he was unused to strange naked children leaping into his arms.

"Kimbery!" she barked. "Get away from him!"

Kimbery clambered down, looking guilty. She probably hadn't intended to disobey. She'd only been caught up in her play.

Still, Avril didn't dare let her think it was acceptable to traffic with Vikings. "Go to bed. Now."

"I didn't mean to."

"Now!"

The little girl began to weep, which made Avril feel awful. After all, she'd been so happy a moment ago. But Avril couldn't afford to let down her guard. Kimbery's life depended upon it.

Tears of heartbreak streamed down Kimmie's face. She started sobbing in earnest and shuffled sadly off to the bedchamber.

Avril bit her lip in remorse. It was hard being a mother. Sometimes she thought she would have had an easier time commanding the army of Rivenloch than she did watching over one wee lass.

But the horrible memory of the berserker hurling his ax into the child's back would never be far away from her thoughts. Kimbery's sobs might tear at her, but at least she was alive to sob.

By the time Avril cleaned up the bath, Kimmie's crying had subsided to sniffles. "Mama?" she called tentatively from the bedchamber. "Come tell me a story."

Avril was tempted to tell her a story about vicious invading savages from the North, to cure her of her misplaced affection for their captive. But she supposed that would give the lass nightmares. Instead, she told her the story of the time she defeated all four of her brothers in combat.

From the next room, Brandr listened in rapt fascination. The woman was telling a grand, typically Pictish tale to her daughter about a warrior wench who'd disguised herself as a man and fought against her own brothers. It was a good story, like the sagas of his people—full of excitement, adventure, and retribution—and the woman had a pleasant voice, lilting and dramatic.

"The first brother, Eldred," she told the little girl, "was very arrogant and boastful."

"Arrogant?" Kimbery asked.

"Like this," she said, and Brandr heard her striding about the room, probably with her arms crossed and her nose in the air. "Anyway, Eldred had never been defeated in battle. So when this new warrior challenged him, he accepted, saluting his foe with a cocky flourish of his blade. They began to fight, exchanging blows back and forth." Brandr could hear her scuffling about and grunting as she recreated the battle with an invisible sword.

"But Eldred was so sure he would win," she said, "that he started to grow careless. And when he relaxed his guard and wasn't paying attention, his sister ducked underneath his arm. With the hilt of her sword, she delivered a hard jab to his chin and knocked him flat."

Kimbery cheered. "What about the other brothers?"

"Grimbol, the second brother, had a nasty temper and was quick to anger. Once he saw Eldred defeated, he immediately drew his sword and rushed in. He meant to slay the warrior who'd dared to humiliate his older brother."

"What's humiliate?"

"Make a fool of. She'd made a fool of his brother, and it made him angry. But his rage proved his own undoing. He began to slash haphazardly and—"

"What's hap-, hap—"

"Haphazardly, in a reckless manner, with poor aim. Most of his blows swished through empty air, and every time he missed, he grew all the more furious. But his sister used his own fury against him. When he lunged at her, she dodged aside and pushed him forward, driving him face-first into the dirt."

Kimbery clapped her hands. "Then what, Mama?"

"The third brother's name was Osbern, and he was a cheat. He'd watched the stranger outwit and outfight his brothers, and he wanted his turn. But instead of waiting for a challenge like a man of honor, he attacked his sister while her back was turned."

Kimbery gasped.

"Oh, she wasn't surprised. She knew all about Osbern's trickery and expected such shameful behavior. She leaped out of the way, and the point of his sword plunged into the mud beside her. Ignoring all the rules of chivalry, he dove at her, intending to wrest her to the ground, where he could pummel her with his fists, like the dishonorable dog that he was. But she was light and quick, and she skipped out of his reach. One clever slice of her sword, and Osbern fell to the sod with his trews around his ankles."

Kimbery giggled. "What about the last brother?"

"When it came time to battle Wilfred, her last brother, the warrior woman tossed off her helm and showed her face."

"Why, Mama?"

"Because Wilfred believed that women were made to be the servants of men, and she wanted him to know exactly who was getting the better of him."

"What did he say when he saw who she was?"

"He called her bad names."

"What bad names?"

"They're so bad, I can't repeat them."

Brandr smiled at that.

"But the other brothers—Eldred, Grimbol, and Osbern—were as angry as bees when they found out they'd been beaten by their own sister. So they yelled at

Wilfred to clout her soundly."

"Oh, nay, Mama."

"But try as he might, Wilfred couldn't lay a hand on her, for she was nimble and strong. You see, while her brothers had lain lazily about, boasting of their skills, she'd spent long hours practicing. She eventually managed to smack his arse with the flat of her sword and sent him crashing into his other brothers."

Kimbery laughed long and hard. "Smack his arse!"

The woman couldn't help but laugh along, which made Brandr grin.

"Aye. And when she'd defeated them all, a servant who'd seen the entire battle ran to tell their father. Her father was so proud of her, he gave her a beautiful jeweled sword as a prize, saying that it was she who should rightfully inherit his lands."

A strange shiver ran up Brandr's spine. He glanced at the jeweled sword in the corner. Could the story be true? Pictish women were said to be able to handle a blade. But could *she* possibly be the intrepid swordswoman in the story? Surely not. Surely the tale was a work of imagination. After all, the heroine of her story had become a landed heiress. This woman lived in a humble hovel.

"Did she live happily ever after, Mama?"

There was a hesitation. "Oh, I'm sure she did."

"Mama," Kimbery announced, "I want a sword."

"You *have* a sword."

Brandr raised a brow. The little girl had a sword?

"Not a wooden sword. A *real* sword," Kimbery said.

"When you're older."

"And I want brothers to fight with," she added.

"That I can't promise you."

"I want to be a warrior just like the lady in the story."

Her mother chuckled. "You'll be twice as good as the lady in the story."

"Mama, can we practice sparring?"

"Tomorrow," she promised, "but only if you get a good night's rest."

After she finished tucking in her daughter, the woman emerged again. Brandr quickly sized her up and decided the story couldn't be true. She might be able to wield a blade, but no sweet-faced maid could possibly vanquish four seasoned warriors.

CHAPTER 6

The next morning, Brandr woke with a face full of sheep. He sputtered and reared back as far as he could, which wasn't far, since he was on a short leash.

"Caimbeul likes you," Kimbery informed him.

He grimaced as the smell of the ewe hit him full force. "Gah!"

"Don't you like her?" she asked.

He blinked the sleep from his eyes. The little girl had obeyed her mother—she was staying out of his reach—but she was holding the sheep on a rope and letting it nuzzle him with its crooked mouth.

"Shouldn't she be outside?" he whispered.

"Shh. Don't tell Mama. She doesn't like when I—"

"Kimmie," came a sleepy voice from the bedchamber. "Who are you talking to?"

"Nobody."

There was a sudden thrash of linens and the woman

rushed into the room, a warning ring in her voice as she came. "You'd better not be going near that Vi-..." When she saw that Kimbery was safe, the anxiety deserted her eyes. Then she saw the ewe. "How did that sheep get in here?"

Kimbery shrugged. "Caimbeul wanted to see my da. I'm going to put her back."

"I've told you a hundred times, Kimmie, sheep don't belong in the house. And he's not your da. Now if you don't take that animal out of here this instant..."

Brandr grew deaf to her scolding as he took note of the woman's attire. By Odin, she was clad in little more than a sheer linen shift, rumpled from sleep. One side had slipped down, exposing the smooth, round cap of her shoulder. There she had a blue tattoo like those engraved on Pict warriors. It was an intriguing three-looped knot that had no beginning or end. Her hair was mussed in a careless way that reminded him of long nights tussling in bed. Her feet were deliciously bare, and her frayed shift revealed the supple curve of her calf and her ankle, which also bore an inked design, this one in the shape of a broken sword. But it was her mouth that was the most alluring. He remembered that mouth now. He'd kissed her, and her lips had been as sweet and soft as wild blackberries.

His loins tightened, and guilt made him grind his teeth against desire. But willing it away didn't make it disappear, and while the woman continued to herd the sheep and her daughter out of the cottage, Brandr fought to keep his thoughts on survival, escape, anything but the beautiful, feminine silhouette revealed by the dawning sun as she opened the door.

Avril silently cursed herself for oversleeping. Keeping Kimbery safe meant being up and about before the wee lass could get herself into trouble. She'd certainly found trouble this morning, letting the ewe into the cottage. Avril wondered if *she'd* been such a handful at that age.

From the doorway, she watched Kimmie lead the sheep back to her pen. "Make sure you close the gate," she called.

Then she turned and caught the Northman staring at her. He looked like a warrior, stern and hardened, about to march into battle. His eyes were hooded, and his jaw was tight. His chest rose and fell with a deep breath as his gaze slowly coursed up the length of her. Finally, he met her eyes.

A flash of heat like lightning seared her as she recognized his expression. She'd been wrong. It wasn't a warrior's bloodlust. It was desire, pure and direct. Her breath caught, and her face turned to flame. But his ice-blue gaze did nothing to quench the fire, instead fueling her distress.

She clenched her fists. She should curse him, clout him, kick him. Yet she did nothing. Though the urge to rebuff him was strong, the compelling lust in his eyes was even stronger.

She licked her lips. Against her will, her gaze drifted down to his mouth. She remembered the light touch of his hands upon her face, the warmth of his breath, the taste of his kiss. What scared her was that a part of her longed to feel it again.

And if Kimbery hadn't burst in upon them at that moment, she didn't know what might have happened.

"Mama! Mama!" Kimbery cried, jumping up and down, waving her wooden sword. "Spar with me! Spar with me!"

Avril cleared her throat. Of course. Sparring had always helped her when she felt emotionally out of sorts. She could take up her sword and slash away at anger, fear, and, in this case, desire, and defeat them soundly before they could get the best of her.

"You promised," Kimbery reminded her.

"I did promise. Just let me get...dressed." A blush stole up her cheek as she realized she'd rushed out in her nightclothes. No wonder the Northman was looking at her like that.

She avoided his gaze as she swept past, but she couldn't avoid hearing the conversation between the Viking and her daughter while she dressed in the next room.

"Do you have a sword?" Kimbery asked.

"I did."

"What happened to it?"

"I lost it in the sea."

"Maybe Mama can get you a new one."

"Kimbery," Avril warned, "are you talking to that man?"

"Nay," she lied. "I'm talking to Maeve."

Avril heard only whispers after that until she emerged.

"Watch me, Da!" Kimbery cried, leaping about with her wooden sword, battling an unseen enemy.

But the Northman's eyes were fixed upon Avril as if nothing else existed.

Brandr's breath caught in his chest. He'd heard legends about female Pict warriors, but he'd never seen a woman dressed, or rather *un*dressed, in such a manner. She'd foregone her confining linen underdress and wore only her sleeveless kirtle, which gave her a greater range of motion and revealed the blue design on her shoulder and her sleek-muscled arms. Riding low on her hips was a leather swordbelt carved with intricate designs. She'd tucked the kirtle back up under the belt so that it bloused halfway down her thighs, exposing a pair of long, lovely legs that were tucked into short seal-fur boots.

If he'd thought the sight of the woman in her nightclothes was alluring, it didn't compare to the vision of her dressed for battle. Perhaps that was the secret of Pict warfare. What foe could fight such a distracting beauty?

"Watch me! Watch me!" the little girl was yelling as she leaped about. It took all of Brandr's willpower to drag his gaze away from the lass's breathtaking mother.

"Kimbery, not in the house," she scolded.

"But I want Da to see me."

"We'll leave the door open." She gave him a look then that said the door would be open, not so he could watch the little girl, but so *she* could keep an eye on *him*.

Which was fine with him. After spending the night on a leash with a throbbing broken arm and waking to a stinking sheep nuzzling at his ear, he figured he deserved the reward of watching a woman cavort about half-naked.

What began as a pleasurable pastime quickly turned into torment. It had been more than a year since Brandr had bedded a woman, and his body responded as eagerly as a starving man seated at a feast. As the woman flexed and lunged in preparation for sparring, she unknowingly taunted him with her taut, slender arms and her silky thighs. Her garment clung to her body, hugging every subtle curve. Each time she twirled to change direction, her skirt flipped up, and he couldn't help but watch for a glimpse of something more.

She hunkered down beside her daughter, giving her instruction, and his gaze slipped over her rounded knees. She wrapped her arms around Kimbery, showing her how to hold the sword, and he observed the nuanced play of the muscles of her shoulder. She stood, planting her feet wide apart, and he admired her shapely calves.

"Can you see me?" Kimbery called out to him.

He gave a guilty start. "Aye," he croaked. The truth was he'd scarcely given her a glance, so transfixed by her mother was he.

"Pay heed, Kimbery," the woman warned. "Don't get distracted."

The little girl began hacking away at her mother with her wooden sword, and the woman easily defended herself, coming around slowly and carefully with her own steel blade. He'd never seen a woman wielding a sword before, and her skill surprised him. He wondered how good she was when she wasn't checking her blows.

Of course, she was no match for a Viking. But it was admirable that she was teaching her daughter useful fighting techniques. It would keep the little girl from becoming easy prey.

He continued to watch as she demonstrated proper shield technique, showed Kimbery how to dodge blows, and the two of them practiced diving to the ground, rolling, and coming up with blades at the ready.

As they sparred, tendrils of the woman's hair came loose from her long braid. Her cheeks grew rosy, her skin glowed, and her chest heaved with each exertion. She reminded him of the women he'd pleasured in his bed when he was a single, virile, carefree young man. He suddenly longed to snatch away her sword, carry her off, toss up her skirts, and ease his desires upon her battle-warmed body. And this troubled him deeply.

Avril found it difficult to concentrate when the Northman was staring at her. She didn't return his stare, but she could feel his eyes upon her. She'd left the door open for more than one reason. Aye, she wanted to keep an eye on him—she was fairly sure he'd already made an attempt to escape—but she also wanted him to see that she was no ordinary frail lass. She could hold her own with a sword. And he'd have a fight on his hands if he tried to challenge her. She'd been a victim once. She didn't intend to be one again.

"Did you see me, Da?" Kimbery yelled after she'd done a perfect forward roll and lunged forward with her wooden sword.

"Aye," he called back, "well done." But his gaze wasn't on Kimbery. He was looking at Avril again with that smoldering heat, like a wolf about to devour a lamb.

She gulped. No one had ever looked at her with such hunger. It made her knees weak and warmed her all over. Curious lightning charged the air, an uncontrollable current born of the strange attraction between them. It sucked the will from her and made her long to do things against her nature—to go to him, to touch him, to kiss him—which terrified her, because her sword was a useless weapon against her own desire.

But fear turned quickly to self-loathing and then fury. Troubled by her wayward emotions and reminding herself that he was her enemy, that his kind had murdered her people and ruined her life, she broke off her gaze and shook free with a shudder, trying to focus again on her lesson with Kimbery.

"Mama, I want to spar with Da," the little girl said, skipping in a circle.

Sweeping her blade sharply through the air, Avril barked, "Don't call him that!"

Kimbery stopped skipping. "What should I call him, Mama?"

Avril could think of a dozen names for the Viking, none fit for the ears of a child. Before she could choose one, he answered.

"Brandr," he called from the cottage. "My name is Brandr."

It was a strong name—a strong name for a strong man. But she didn't want to know his name. Knowing his

name made things worse. He was easy to despise when he was simply a Viking, a Northman, a marauder. Calling him Brandr made him a man of flesh and blood.

"Can Brandr fight with us, Mama?"

"Nay."

"Why not?" Kimmie asked.

He answered before she had a chance. "I wouldn't want to hurt you, little one."

Avril smirked at that. "He's afraid he might lose."

Brandr lifted a brow and gave her a cocky smile. "Not even with a broken arm."

His grin sent a shiver through her. She hoped it was a shiver of revulsion. She feared it was something else, something that made her feel lightheaded and foolhardy, almost crazy enough to free him and let him try...almost.

But she wasn't a fool. She couldn't let him bait her.

"My name's Kimmie," Kimbery informed him, holding her sword high over her head. "And Mama's name is Avril."

Avril choked. She didn't want him to know her name. The exchange of names suggested an intimacy she didn't want to encourage.

"Pleased to meet you, Kimmie," he said with a polite nod. *Her* name, however, came out on a purr. "Avril."

She bristled. That was exactly why she'd wished to remain nameless. Already he breathed her name as if they were lovers. Already it felt like he was insinuating his way under her skin.

"Come on, Kimmie," she said, shaking off the uneasy shiver that had passed through her. "Let's show the

Viking what we do to men who think they can hurt us."

She hoped to impress upon him that the ladies of Rivenloch were not to be trifled with or underestimated. But she also worried that his shipmates might show up. So she taught Kimbery some useful defensive ploys in addition to straightforward sword fighting. She showed her how to use her elbows to jab a belly, her heels to stamp on toes, her teeth to bite fingers, and her fists to punch a man where it hurt most.

So enrapt was she with teaching Kimbery survival skills that she didn't notice the figure stealing up on the cottage until it was too late. But the instant she saw the glint of metal, her worst fears were realized. It could be no one else. The Northman's shipmates must have come looking for him.

Without a second glance, she swung Kimbery up and pushed her toward the cottage door. "Go!"

For once, Kimbery didn't question her, but rushed inside.

Her Viking prisoner, however, called out, "Is it my men?"

She didn't answer him. She wouldn't give him the satisfaction. Wheeling immediately with her blade drawn and her heart racing, she faced the oncoming threat.

But it wasn't his men. It was her neighbor, the one who'd given her the sheep. She lowered her shoulders in relief. While she watched the man make his way toward her, she saw that he wielded, not a sword, but a spade.

"Erik!" Brandr called out suddenly from behind her. "Gunnarr!"

Her eyes widened. Shite! She couldn't let her neighbor find the Northman.

She whipped her head around and hissed at him. "Hush! It's not your men!"

The last thing she saw before she lunged for the door, slamming it shut, was the perplexed furrow between the Viking's brows.

Brandr bellowed out a curse. Unfortunately, he startled the little girl, who now looked as if she might burst into tears.

"Shh, Kimmie. I'm sorry," he soothed. "It's all right."

But he wasn't so sure. He wished the woman hadn't slammed the door between them. If it wasn't his men out there, who was it? Thieves? Murderers? Though he realized it was completely contrary to reason at the moment—Avril was his enemy, after all—his instinct to protect women rose to the surface, overriding everything else. Whoever was out there evidently posed a threat to her. Otherwise, she wouldn't have pushed Kimbery into the cottage.

He had to do something about it.

Kimbery's chin was trembling, and the wooden sword drooped in her grasp. "But Mama..."

"Hush, Kimmie," he coaxed. "It's all right. Shh."

"I have to help Mama fight," she decided, starting for the door.

"Nay!" She flinched at his sharp voice. "Nay, sweetheart," he said more softly. "Your mama wants you to stay here, to stay quiet. That's why she closed the door."

Yet even as he said the words, he had to wonder at the

woman's judgment. Why hadn't she rushed inside as well and barred the door? What made her think she could handle the threat? The fool woman was going to get herself killed.

Hell, he thought as he strained against the leather collar, he couldn't stand the thought of a woman facing danger alone while he sat helpless. If only he could get loose, he could chase the intruders off.

He glanced at the little girl. Maybe he *could* get loose.

"Kimmie," he said, "if you help *me,* I can help your mama."

She looked skeptically at him.

"I need you to unbuckle my collar. Do you think you can do that? Do you think you can—"

"Mama said I'm not supposed to go near you."

Brandr bit back an oath. "But she needs my help. I'm big and strong, and I can fight—"

"*I'm* strong," she said. "Mama said so."

He growled in frustration, frightening the little girl again. She backed toward the door once more.

His eyes widened. "Nay, nay, nay, nay, nay." He had to keep her inside. The last thing he needed was to have *both* women out of his sight. "Kimmie, nay, Kimmie," he said urgently as her small hand touched the latch. "Come away from the door. Please. I'll..." He searched his memory. What would have convinced his own daughter to stay? "I'll tell you another story."

She hesitated.

"Aye, come sit by the fire, and I'll tell you a story about...about Muspell, the land of the Fire Giants."

She pursed her lips.

"And Niflheim, where the Frost Giants live," he added.

She lifted her brows.

"And Audhumia, the giant cow."

"Giant cow?"

"Aye. The giant cow who licked the gods to life."

She let go of the latch and walked to the hearth, and he heaved a sigh of relief. He might not be able to rescue Avril, but at least he could keep her daughter safe.

Kimbery sat cross-legged with her sword across her lap, and he began a story he'd told often to his children—the story of the world's creation. Meanwhile, he strained to hear what was happening outside, to no avail. The little girl, fascinated by the tale, edged closer and closer to him. Eventually, despite her mother's stern orders, she ended up half-draped across his lap.

CHAPTER 7

A vril thought she must be mad, covering for the Northman. Her neighbor said he'd found pieces of a Viking ship. He'd come to warn her to be watchful, assuring her in manly tones that he was on the hunt for the vermin who belonged to it, hefting up his spade as proof.

She should have turned the Viking over to him then and there. It certainly would have made her life easier. Brandr would have been out of her house, away from her daughter, off of her shoulders.

But she couldn't bear the thought of him being beaten to death with a spade, which was doubtless what her neighbor intended.

So she told the man an outright lie, saying she'd seen no sign of Northmen, but she'd be sure to alert him if she did. Thanking him for his concern, she smiled stiffly until he was out of sight.

"Brilliant," she muttered to herself. "Now I'm harboring an outlaw."

She pushed open the cottage door, cursing herself for a fool, and froze when she saw the scene before her.

She couldn't draw breath. Mother of God, she *was* a fool! While she'd been lying to protect him, the crafty Viking had enticed her daughter onto his lap. Kimbery was sprawled across his thighs like a lovesick pup. Was this the thanks she got for saving Brandr's worthless hide?

"Mama!" Kimbery cried, jumping up and running to her, hugging her about the thighs. "Da's telling me...I mean, Brandr's telling me a story about a giant cow and Frost Giants and the dwarves who hold up the sky!"

"Is that so?" Avril bit out with a shaky smile for her daughter. She clasped Kimbery close in relief, grateful he'd let her go, unharmed, but uncertain why. After all, with Kimbery in his grasp, he could have had her at his mercy and easily bargained for his freedom.

Brandr didn't seem to notice her confusion. He gave her a fierce frown, scanning her from head to toe. "Are you all right?"

She blinked, even more baffled. "Aye. Why wouldn't I be?"

"Who was outside?" The furrow in his brow deepened, and his fists clenched, as if he meant to use them.

"My neighbor. He came to tell me..." Suddenly the truth struck her. "Were you...?" She narrowed incredulous eyes at him. "You were. You were afraid for me."

He scowled in irritation, but he couldn't deny it, and something about that pleased her.

"You know," she said in amazement, "if I didn't know better, I'd say you were trying to protect me."

He scoffed. But after a moment he looked at her quizzically, lowering his shoulders and relaxing his hands. "Wait. Your neighbor?" The corner of his lip lifted in a knowing grin. "And you didn't tell him about your Viking prize?"

She stiffened.

He chuckled. "You know, if I didn't know better, I'd say you were trying to protect me."

It was useless to deny it.

He shook his head. "What a pair we are."

What a pair indeed, Avril thought. By all rights, they should despise each other. The war between their people had been going on for more than fifty years. He was a bloodthirsty Viking, and she was the Pict who'd leashed him. She'd made the cottage that he'd come to conquer into his prison. And if they'd met on a field of battle, she would have readily drawn her sword and stabbed him through the heart.

But when she looked at his twinkling blue eyes, his enticing grin, his...formidable body, she found it hard to summon up a good loathing.

"Mama, did you smack his arse?"

Avril started. "Who, the neighbor?" She shook her head. "He wasn't here to fight. He...came to see how Caimbeul was doing."

"Oh."

She and Brandr exchanged glances, and he gave her a subtle nod of thanks, something she wasn't sure she

deserved. She was making a mistake, not turning him in. The longer he was here, the more difficult it would become to get rid of him. Hell, her own daughter was already clambering onto the Viking's lap as if he were her beloved grandfather.

Kimbery hopped up and down on her toes. "Mama, I want a giant cow!"

Avril eyed the Northman in accusation. What nonsense had he put in Kimbery's head now?

Brandr reasoned with the little girl. "But how would you milk her? It would take all day. And your hands are too small."

"You could do it," Kimbery suggested. "You have big hands."

Avril bit her lip. He *did* have big hands...and big feet...and big shoulders...

He chuckled. "I'm not a milkmaid," he told Kimmie. "I'm a warrior."

His words suddenly touched a raw nerve in Avril. She wasn't a milkmaid either. She was supposed to be the lady of a castle. But sometimes the world turned on people, and they had to do what was necessary to go on living.

"You know, not all of us get to choose our fate," and she said with frost in her voice. "If you're going to stay here, you'd better get used to tending animals and fishing and mending fences. It's not an easy thing, surviving in..."

She broke off at his narrowed gaze, realizing what she'd just said—*if you're going to stay here.*

What was she thinking? He wasn't an animal she could

tame and tether. He was a wild and dangerous beast who'd surely turn on her the moment he was free.

Still, he could have hurt Kimbery, but he'd chosen not to. Instead he'd told the little girl some fanciful tale about giant cows to keep her quiet and safe from whatever peril lurked outside.

Why? Did he hope to persuade her to let him go? She couldn't do that. She might not deliver him directly into the hands of a neighbor armed with a spade, but neither would she turn a known marauder loose on her unsuspecting countrymen.

Kimbery waved her wooden blade through the air. "My mama's a warrior," she said. "And I'm going to be a warrior, too. When I grow up, we're going to take back Rivenloch."

"Kimmie!" Avril's cheeks warmed. She didn't need a stranger knowing all about her sordid past. "He's not interested in—"

"What's Rivenloch?" he asked.

"It's Mama's castle. I'm going to learn how to sword fight, and then we'll get an army to take the castle back from my evil uncles who—"

"Kimmie, enough! Go take your nap."

Kimbery scampered merrily off into the bedchamber. But the damage was already done. Brandr was staring at her with undisguised interest now. "Evil uncles?"

Though he'd entertained the remote possibility, it hadn't seriously occurred to Brandr that the woman and her daughter were anything but commoners, outcasts on this lonely shore due to an unfortunate encounter with berserkers.

He perused her thoroughly now, imagining her in the rich garb of a noblewoman. It wasn't difficult.

"It's only a tale," she muttered, "an invention like your giant cows and...and snow ogres."

"Frost Giants," he corrected. She wasn't a very good liar. "And the story of Audhumla is true."

She crossed her arms and smirked at him. "Really? Dwarves?"

He frowned. "How do *you* think the sky stays up?"

She shook her head as she propped her sword in the corner.

Though she tried to make light of it, Brandr couldn't let go of the feeling that there was more than a morsel of truth to her story.

Avril had had ample opportunity to kill him, even the chance to turn him over to someone else to kill. And yet she hadn't. She'd had mercy on him—feeding him, sheltering him, tending to his broken arm—when anyone else would have let him suffer. Though he was her enemy, she'd treated him with respect, wisdom, fairness, and honor. She seemed to have been raised as he had—with the qualities necessary to inspire followers and command warriors. It wasn't hard to imagine she was that woman who'd fought for the jeweled sword, that her four brothers were Kimbery's evil uncles, and that they'd taken advantage of her misfortune to seize her inheritance from her.

He and Avril must both be cursed by the gods then. He'd lost his family, his men, and his ship. She'd lost her innocence, her birthright, and her land. They were kindred souls. Against his better judgment, he found he wanted to know more about this intrepid woman.

"So in that...story...you told your daughter," he asked as she stirred the banked embers on the hearth to life with a stick, "where is this Rivenloch?"

She shrugged. "It's an imaginary place."

"Your daughter doesn't seem to think so."

She arched a slim brow at him. "My daughter thinks she's a selkie, her sheep talks to her, and you're her father."

She had a point. "But you *are* teaching her to fight with a sword."

"Aye, so she can protect herself from..." She gave him a fleeting glance, and he was sure she intended to say "Vikings." Instead she substituted, "Attackers."

He nodded. "Where did you learn to fight?"

"All Pictish women know how to fight," she said proudly. "Don't Viking women know how to fight?"

"There's no need. They have Viking men to protect them."

"Indeed?" She gave him a cursory perusal, as if she were sizing up a horse. "And who protects them from the Viking men?"

He scowled when he realized she was serious.

Avril had felt the Northman's iron grip on her wrist. She'd seen his bulging muscles. He had the shoulders of an ox and was at least a head taller than anyone she knew. What was to keep a man like him from taking what he wanted from a woman?

"The law protects them," he replied at last, as if it were obvious.

"The law," she scoffed. "You mean the law that *men* make and enforce?"

"Men *and* women."

She lifted a skeptical brow.

He frowned. "Is it not so here? Do you not have an *althing?*"

"*Althing?*"

"A meeting of all the villagers." She waited for him to continue. "A meeting where the rules are made." At her silence, he added, "By everyone."

"*All* the villagers?" she asked doubtfully.

"Anyone who wishes to attend."

"Men *and* women?"

"Of course."

That gave Avril pause. She gazed wistfully into the fire, wishing it were thus with her people as well. Her father had understood. He'd believed that women were just as capable as men. That was why he'd made her his heir. But most men were like her brothers, who thought that a woman's place was under a man's boot.

"In my land," Brandr added softly, "the warrior woman in your story? She would never have lost her castle."

Avril bit her lip.

He continued. "Anyone who refused her rule would have been sent into exile."

Her throat tightened. That was how it should have been. Instead, *she'd* been sent into exile.

He went on. "And she wouldn't need an army to take back what was rightfully hers."

Tears of frustration threatened behind her eyes, but she bit them back. She couldn't think about that. What was past was past. She couldn't change what had happened. And there was nothing she could do about it now.

Mortified at the thought of crying in front of a Viking, she sniffed sharply, clapped the soot from her hands, and abruptly stood up. Unfortunately, as she did so, she stepped on the hem of her skirt, which was still partially tucked into her belt. In the blink of an eye, she tripped and stumbled sideways toward the fire.

How Brandr moved so swiftly, she didn't know. In one instant, she was falling face-first toward the burning coals, and in the next, he'd caught her with his boot and propelled her back toward him.

As she fell, she reflexively put out her hands. She managed to partially catch herself, though she heard him grunt in pain as she fell against his splinted arm. But that wasn't the worst of it. She landed with her hands on his chest, her face in his belly, and her breast in his palm.

CHAPTER 8

Brandr hardly felt the throbbing in his broken arm. It was nothing compared to the panicked throbbing of his heart. The woman had almost fallen into the fire. Thank Odin he'd had the reflexes and strength to save her. "Are you all right?"

She lifted her head to look up at him. There was a curious expression on her face, as if she were simultaneously relieved and horrified.

Then he realized what part of her was nestled against his palm, and suddenly the throbbing of his arm and his heart diminished in comparison to the burgeoning throbbing in his trousers. It had been a long time since he'd felt the soft fullness of a woman's breast. His response was unavoidable.

They stared at each other uncertainly, knowing they had to extricate themselves from this awkward predicament somehow, both reluctant to move for fear of making it worse. The moment stretched on, becoming more and more strained, and neither budged.

And then a strange thing happened. Avril closed her eyes and made a small sound in her throat, not quite a sigh of pleasure, not quite a whimper of distress, and her fingers tightened with subtle pressure on his chest. He froze, afraid to breathe.

When she opened her eyes again, it was only halfway, and she lowered her gaze to his mouth. He, too, was drawn to her lips—so sweet, so tempting, like ripe fruit just out of his reach.

He had the mad urge to lean down and steal a kiss, to taste her soft, succulent lips once again, to be reckless and bold and claim her like a marauder.

But the damned leather collar around his neck prevented him.

Hell, it was just as well. After all, it would be a mistake to do something so impulsive and irresponsible. It would destroy her trust and ruin his plans for escape.

He had to resist temptation.

She, however, didn't even try.

Lust knocked Avril over like an unexpected ocean wave, stealing her breath away, dragging her into deeper currents, drowning her good sense.

In some dim corner of her brain, she knew she should back away. But Brandr's chest felt deliciously strong and supple beneath her fingers. His breath caressed her brow. His eyes were smoky and inviting. What she really wanted to do was kiss him.

She eased forward the slightest bit, sucking in a quick breath as his hand rasped gently across her breast. She hesitated, then moved against him again, relishing the tantalizing friction as his palm grazed her. The third time, she squeezed her eyes shut in pleasure. And he responded, moving his thumb tenderly across her nipple.

There was no stopping the coursing tide then. With a soft gasp, she surged forward, caught his stubbled face between her hands, and planted her lips across his enticing mouth.

His cheek was coarse, he smelled of smoke and the sea, and his body was as hard and rough as seasoned oak. But his lips were warm and yielding, and his kiss was filled with gentle wonder.

He answered her at once, angling his face to release and recapture her lips, drawing them in with his own. He breathed passion across her cheek and gasped as she licked experimentally at his mouth. His jaw opened in invitation, and for an instant she hesitated, wondering if he'd bite her like that wolf in his story. Then yearning overrode caution, and she let her tongue venture within, enjoying the ale-sweet taste of him and the pleasing shock as his tongue answered in kind.

Her eager fingers furrowed through his hair, unmindful of his salt-crusted tangles. She pressed closer, letting her breasts chafe provocatively against his chest. They were both breathing heavily now, and she could feel her heart beating like the ocean pounding the shore.

She continued to kiss him, in too deep to turn back. She dared not stop to take a breath, for fear one of them might come to their senses and halt the exhilarating madness.

His soft groan, deep in his throat, was like the purr of a

great wild animal, and it sent a frisson of strange current through her, as if he'd called to her. Lightning coursed through her body and struck at the place she most longed to be touched—that burning ember between her thighs.

He seemed to know instantly what she needed. His hand found her, even through her skirts, cupping her with a firm precision that made her gasp. She shivered as he rubbed slowly against her, easing and provoking her at the same time.

She squeezed her eyes tightly. This was mad. It was wrong. And yet it felt so right. She couldn't seem to stop. His body was a strong lodestone, and she was drawn to him like a powerless scrap of iron.

He opened her mouth wider with his, thrusting his tongue inside, devouring her, and she feasted equally on him. Her nipples stung where they brushed across his chest. And where his fingers now delved with more intense finesse, she began to swell with longing.

Desire rose like an incoming tide, too swift to escape, and soon she was swept off her feet. Higher and higher she was carried on a wave of lust, out of control, unsure of her destiny, led by a stranger. And yet she was helpless to resist.

Brandr was past thought. Otherwise, he'd never have put himself in this situation. This was the woman who had knocked him out and tied him up, and what was he doing? Pleasuring her.

Of course, she wasn't the only one receiving pleasure. It had been a long while since he'd enjoyed the attentions of a woman so enthusiastic and forthright, a woman who

lustily took what she wanted. But his body hadn't forgotten how to respond to such enthusiasm.

He naturally let her have her way.

He let her kiss him like a greedy suckling lamb. He let her explore his body, run her fingers over his chest and through his hair. He let her press the supple pillows of her breasts against him. He let her arch against his hand, begging wordlessly for his touch.

And he answered her onslaught with the instinctive cravings of his love-starved body.

Blood rushed through his veins and roared in his ears as their tongues entwined and their breath mingled. Even through the layers of linen, the tempting crevice between her legs was impossibly hot, and he ached to plunge there with more than just his fingers.

Indeed, the lusty beast in his trousers was rousing, growing more demanding and frustrated by the moment. And the fact that satisfaction was so close, yet unattainable, drove him even more mad.

What made him open his eyes, he didn't know— maybe a warrior's innate sense of his surroundings. But the flicker of peripheral movement made him freeze.

The sudden tension in his body instantly alerted her as well. She stiffened, her lips still clinging to his.

"Mama!" came the little girl's scolding voice from the doorway. "I told you a hundred times, don't go near that bad man!"

Avril's eyes went wide, and she pulled away in horror, struggling to her feet and stammering. "I...I...I..."

Since she seemed too tongue-tied to come up with a

reasonable explanation, Brandr offered one. "Your mama fell," he said, which was true.

"Aye," Avril choked out, straightening her garments. "I fell."

The little girl eyed them uncertainly, and Brandr held his breath, waiting. Then Kimbery shrugged and skipped off to the kitchen, plopped down on her stool and began chattering to her doll.

The air was heavy with unrequited desire, and the tension between Avril and him was as taut as a drawn bowstring. He didn't dare speak or even glance at her for fear of rekindling the volatile spark between them. It seemed like an eternity before his hunger subsided and he could draw an even breath.

Avril couldn't look at the Northman. She pressed her fingertips into her brow, hiding her eyes behind her hands in shame.

What had she done?

Hell, she'd let him kiss her, hold her, touch her. She'd shown weakness to her enemy, let him gain the upper hand, surrendered to his seduction. But she couldn't let him believe that he'd won some victory over her, that she was somehow vulnerable to him.

Making sure Kimbery was occupied and avoiding Brandr's gaze, she hunkered down to poke at the fire and whispered sharply, "Never do that again."

He barked out an incredulous chuckle, then whispered back, "What—save you from falling into the fire?"

Her lips thinned. "Kiss me," she whispered. "Never kiss me again."

He scoffed, then whispered, "I believe it was *you* who kissed *me*."

Her face grew hot at the truth of his words, but she didn't dare back down. "An honorable man would never make such..." The words stuck in her throat as she remembered the glorious sensation of his hand between her legs. "Such bold advances toward an unwilling woman."

He murmured, "I don't recall you being unwilling at all."

She gasped, casting an anxious glance at Kimbery.

"In fact," he continued, "I'm collared and bound and chained to the wall. It isn't as if I had a choice in the matter."

It was true, of course. She'd thrown herself at him. But he didn't have to come out and say it.

She felt thoroughly humiliated now. She'd made a fool of herself, attacking him with the same raw aggression she'd used on her lovers in that shameful period after her rape. Only this was much worse. This time she'd forced herself upon a man with no power to resist her. Hell, she was no better than the berserker who'd violated her.

Was that why she'd thrown herself at Brandr? Was she somehow seeking revenge upon him for what another of his kind had done to her?

As much as it pained her to admit it, she feared it might be true. She'd treated the Northman with undeserved disrespect. She owed him an apology. Swallowing hard and closing her eyes, she mumbled, "You're right. It was dishonorable of me. I'm sorry."

After what seemed an interminable length of time, he breathed, "I'm not."

Their glances collided then. And in that moment that caught them both off-guard, they were no longer Viking and Pict, no longer prisoner and captor, but man and woman.

What had made Brandr admit the truth about how he felt, he didn't know. It was reckless and unwise. The more emotionally entangled he became with this woman, the harder it would be to betray her and make his escape.

But he couldn't deny he felt...something...for the fiery Pictish lass. What troubled him was that it might be something deeper than just physical lust.

Lust he could deal with. It made sense, after all. He'd been without a woman for so long, it was only natural his body should respond at the first available opportunity. But if it were something more...

By Thor, he had to get out of this mess!

Avril, obviously discomfited by his confession, backed away and ushered Kimbery outside, ostensibly to gather cockles, but probably also to get a breath of fresh, sobering air.

While they were gone, Brandr worked at the iron ring, pulling and twisting to try to loosen it from the mortared stone. The woman might not have turned him in to her neighbor this morn, but that didn't mean she wouldn't ever. Even if she relished the idea of having captured a Viking, even if she enjoyed lording it over him as her prisoner, even if she found amusement and pleasure in his arms, eventually she'd tire of it...and him.

He shouldn't have encouraged her. True, he was collared and bound and unable to avoid her caresses. But he could have turned a cold countenance to her. He could have refused to bend to her seductive will. He could have clamped his mouth shut and made fists of his hands.

Instead, in an instant of weakness, he'd ignored reason. He'd let himself be tempted by her feminine desire, allowed himself to drift with her on an erotic sea. And for one moment, he'd almost believed that they were kindred souls floating there, that they shared a common destination and a deeper destiny.

But he had to ignore such feelings. It would only make things more difficult when the time came to play the traitor.

He yanked hard at the collar, bruising his throat. The iron ring wouldn't budge. He cursed and slumped back against the wall. How much longer did he have? How much longer would it be before Avril decided he was a bad influence on her daughter and a danger to her? How much longer before she turned him in?

CHAPTER 9

Before she even opened her eyes the following morning, Avril could hear them in the next room—Brandr murmuring, Kimbery giggling. It was a pleasant sound, a sound that reminded her of what it was like to have a real family. Her lips curved up as foolish, sentimental tears brimmed in her eyes.

She'd told herself she didn't need family. Her parents were dead. Her brothers had betrayed her. And there was little hope of her finding a husband, since she had nothing to offer. She'd convinced herself that Kimbery was family enough.

But the truth was Avril was terribly lonely.

Most days, she kept herself too busy to notice. Her mind she occupied with survival. Her heart she occupied with Kimbery.

Still, regret occasionally crept in, and she grieved for the person she used to be—the young woman who was meant to reign over a noble keep, marry a strong warrior, and have a dozen beautiful children. Most of the time that regret manifested as a righteous thirst for justice and a determination to get back what belonged to her. But sometimes, like this morn, a melancholy pining welled up in her, and she ached for what she couldn't have.

She definitely couldn't have Brandr. There was no question about that. He might have felt right in her arms. His kiss might have been sweet and tempting. His hands might have touched her with the deceptive devotion of a lover. But he was her enemy.

Barbarians like him had invaded her land for decades now. They'd razed her villages, stolen her coin, slaughtered her people. One of them had killed her father and raped her. They were brutal, ruthless savages, and they were beyond reason.

Why then was it so impossible to imagine the whispering Viking in the next room wielding an axe and charging unarmed Pictish children?

Kimbery giggled again, and this time she was joined by the Northman. His laugh was deep and warm, and it sent delicious shivers along Avril's arms.

She swallowed hard and opened her eyes to stare at the ceiling.

What in God's name was she going to do with Brandr?

She couldn't turn him in. She didn't have the heart to deliver him into the hands of an angry mob. Hell, she'd already proven that—hiding him from the man who'd come yesterday.

But she couldn't let him go either. If anything

happened to her neighbors because she'd set a Viking loose, she'd never be able to live with herself.

And she couldn't keep him tied up forever. She might be a formidable foe, but she wasn't inhumane.

In the midst of agonizing over what to do with the Northman, she heard Kimbery's giggles interrupted abruptly by a low thud, a silent pause, and then a thin wail.

Avril's heart stopped. Fearing the worst, she thrashed to get free of the tangle of sheets. Cursing her own clumsiness as Kimbery's voice rose to a piercing cry, Avril tripped beside the bed, landing on one knee, her foot still caught in the linens.

What had he done to her? What had that damned Viking done to her little girl?

Fear sucked her mouth dry. It seemed to take forever before she finally managed to get free of the bedclothes and shot to her feet.

She'd kill him! She'd kill the bastard for making her daughter cry.

Desperate to reach Kimbery, she rushed forward, tripping over Kimbery's cloth doll on the floor and catching herself as she slammed against the bedchamber wall.

At last stumbling through the doorway, she froze at the sight, her eyes wide.

Kimbery was sobbing on Brandr's shoulder, and his head was inclined toward hers as he murmured soothing words against her hair.

The protective mother in Avril wanted to snatch Kimbery away at once.

But before she had a chance to move, Brandr met her gaze over Kimbery's head, and she instantly saw the truth in his compassionate eyes. He hadn't hurt Kimbery. She'd hurt herself. And she'd run to him for comfort.

Avril didn't know what to think. Kimbery had been far too trusting of the Northman, sharing her doll with him, drawing pictures of him, listening to his stories, calling him Da. And yet sometimes children had an instinct for people. Sometimes they could tell who was good and who was bad.

She stood at the doorway, watching them in tense silence.

Kimbery's sobbing subsided to sniffles, and she lifted her head to look at Brandr. "Is it bleeding?"

He narrowed his eyes, studying her brow. "A bit."

Kimbery touched the place and drew her fingers away, whimpering at the sight of the blood on her fingertips.

"It should make a fine scar," he assured her. "All great warriors have battle scars."

She stopped crying. "They do?"

"Aye."

"Do you have a scar?"

"Oh, aye, lots of them."

"Where?"

"There's one here, under my chin." He lifted his chin for her to see, though it was covered with stubble. Then he lowered his head. "And I have one on my forehead, like you."

"Did you run into a table, too?"

"Nay." He tried to scowl, but his eyes were twinkling. "That's where Thor struck me with a bolt of lightning."

"Really?"

His frown melted into a smile. "Nay, not really. My brother caught my brow with an axe."

"Is your brother evil like my mama's brothers?"

Avril's breath caught.

"Nay," he said. "It was an accident. We were sparring."

After a thoughtful moment, Kimbery rose to press a kiss to his brow. Avril's jaw dropped. "Mama says this will make it all better. Now you give mine a kiss."

Before Avril could gasp out a word, Kimbery leaned her head toward Brandr's lips, giving him no choice but to repay the gesture.

When Kimbery pulled away, she cocked her head and touched a finger to his temple, where Avril had clubbed him with the driftwood. "Is that a battle scar?"

A hint of a smile threatened at the corner of his lips. "Aye."

"My mama has a battle scar."

Avril nearly choked.

Kimbery continued, "It's right here." She pointed to the right side of her chest.

Brandr's smile blossomed into a full grin. "Really?'

Avril had heard enough. Blushing, she swept into the room. "Kimbery, what happened?"

Kimbery jumped up and ran to her. "Mama, I have a battle scar!"

"Is that so?" She crouched to inspect Kimbery's brow. There was a red bump and a tiny cut there, so tiny that

she'd be surprised if it left any mark at all. Nonetheless, she frowned in concern. "And who were you battling to give you such a scar?"

"Sir...Table!"

"I see." She ruffled the top of Kimbery's hair. "And did you give Sir Table battle scars as well?"

Kimbery nodded and then leaned against her and began twining her fingers in Avril's hair. "Mama, I let Brandr kiss my cut."

And I let him kiss my lips, Avril thought. But all she said was, "Oh?"

Kimbery added in a loud whisper, "I don't think he's a very bad man."

Avril sighed, and she felt the tension go out of her. Kimbery was right. He wasn't a very bad man. He'd done nothing wrong. In spite of being shipwrecked and captured and tied up, he'd been civil and even kind. He'd told Kimbery stories, he'd eased away her tears, and been a model father to a little girl who'd never had one. He'd even saved Avril from falling into the fire. Avril slowly raised her gaze over Kimbery's shoulder and looked him squarely in the eye. "Neither do I."

Brandr should have been relieved. Avril was staring at him with complete trust now. He could tell by her eyes that she had no intention of turning him in. He wouldn't have to worry about escaping, because she wouldn't tell anyone he was here. She meant to set him free.

To his surprise, his heart sank. As mad as it was, despite his broken arm, his banged-up nose, and the cursed dog collar around his neck, he'd rather enjoyed the past few days. Avril was a fascinating woman—spirited and passionate, sensitive yet strong, and her daughter was delightful. Now that the opportunity for escape was at hand, he wasn't sure he wanted to leave.

The way she was looking at him made his heart melt. Ever since he'd lost his wife and children, there had been a deep, hollow abyss in his soul. Losing his ship and his men had thrown him farther into the chasm and made it seem impossible to ever reach the surface. But between Avril's kindhearted honor and Kimbery's innocent adoration, he'd started to believe that he could climb out of that hole, that he might be capable of caring and loving again.

Kimbery pushed away from her mother suddenly and galloped across the room into the bedchamber, announcing, "Look at me! I'm a Valkyrie!"

Avril looked askance at him, and he lifted one corner of his lip in a sheepish half-smile.

She came to hunker down beside him then, to tell him what he already knew. "I've decided I won't turn you in."

He waited in silence, not sure he wanted to hear the rest.

She turned in profile to him and lowered her eyes. "My father taught me not to judge a man by the sins of his brothers." She took a deep breath and let it out on a sigh. "You may have Viking blood in your veins. But you have nothing in common with the man who attacked me."

He held his breath, like a felon awaiting his sentence.

"I'm not sure what I'm going to do with you yet," she admitted, "but after all you've done for Kimbery...and for me..." Her glance flickered momentarily to his lips, and he knew she was remembering their kiss. *He* was remembering their kiss. He wished she would kiss him again. She tucked her lower lip under her teeth, then lifted love-soft eyes to his. "I vow I won't let harm come to you."

The naked reverence in her beautiful amber eyes took Brandr's breath away. No woman had ever regarded him with such forthright fondness or gifted him with such a heartfelt promise. The way she was looking at him made him feel he could do anything, even crawl out of his dark underworld into the light.

He opened his mouth to blurt something in return—he wasn't sure what—probably something foolish and maudlin. But Kimbery shot suddenly back through the doorway, and Avril steered her into the kitchen to prepare breakfast.

Part of him felt relief. He'd been racked with guilt all this time, cursing his misplaced affections for Avril as some weakness on his part. To know that she felt the same way about him—that her feelings went deeper than lust, that she recognized his good heart, and that she genuinely cared about him—lifted his spirits.

But the other part of him, the rational part, realized that there was one thing he feared more than Avril turning him in. And that was Avril trying to keep him safe.

Her trusting gaze filled him with dread. There had been much more than simple mercy in her expression. He'd glimpsed a dangerous combination of affection and determination in her eyes, the same unflinching adoration and steely will that had kept her daughter alive on this barren spit of shore.

The fact was she didn't want him to leave either. As improbable as it seemed, the two of them—captive and captor, mortal enemies—had somehow done much more than find common ground and an uneasy peace. They'd fallen in love. And now she naively believed she could keep him.

But she couldn't, not without endangering herself and her daughter. She couldn't hide him. Anyone with one good eye could see Brandr was a Viking. She'd never be able to explain how he'd arrived here, where he'd come from, how they'd met.

And he knew what would happen after that. Avril would be called a Viking sympathizer, branded a traitor, and probably executed. And Brandr wouldn't be able to do a damned thing to protect her.

He was cursed. Misfortune befell anyone who got close to him. As much as his heart ached with the desire to stay, as much as he knew he'd be hurled back into his familiar pit of despair if he left, he knew the only answer was to ignore the bittersweet yearning in his soul, turn his back on her—on both of them, and go.

CHAPTER 10

A vril swept through the seagrass toward the bleating ewe, a stool under one arm and her milk bucket bouncing against her thigh. She felt as light as thistledown atop a bubbling stream. She didn't have all the details worked out, but she knew that sparing Brandr's life was the right decision.

He was a decent man. Maybe he was a Viking, and maybe he'd come as an invader, but he'd shown her nothing but humanity, courtesy, and kindness, in spite of her hostility. He'd seen to Kimbery's cut and kept her from harm by telling her stories. He'd saved Avril from fire and feared for her welfare when she'd confronted her neighbor. It was obvious he felt protective of them.

Did he feel something more? Her heart fluttered at the possibility, and she grew slightly giddy, remembering the way he'd looked at her just now, not only with relief and gratitude, but with a sweet sort of devotion.

She couldn't help but smile as she pushed through the

gate and closed it behind her. Plopping the stool down next to Caimbeul, she seated herself. She rested her palm on the animal's flank and set the bucket under the sheep's belly. As she milked the ewe, she daydreamed.

What if Brandr stayed here with her, with them? He had nowhere else to go, after all. His men hadn't shown up. He was a stranger in her land. He was a castaway, stranded here with no means of survival. She could offer him a roof over his head, food, safety...and perhaps something more.

She leaned her brow against the sheep's woolly side and closed her eyes.

What if the attraction she felt for him grew into genuine love? Could he be a father for Kimbery? And— she dared to imagine—could he be a husband to *her?*

Three days ago, she would have thought it impossible. Now it seemed not only possible, but right. After all, they were both castoffs, exiled from their people. It seemed natural and fitting to seek comfort in each other's company.

She squeezed the last milk from the ewe's udders and retrieved the bucket before giving the sheep a pat to send her trotting across the pasture. Then she sat there for a moment, gazing up at the sky, where low morning clouds made a soft gray blanket that would dissolve away by midday.

Staring into the heavens, she made up her mind. She was going to let him go, set him free. In fact, she'd unleash him right now.

It was risky, she thought as she made her way back to

the cottage. Once he was loose, he could physically hurt her, or he could run out of her life forever.

But she didn't think he'd do either. He'd had ample opportunity to do her and Kimbery harm, and he'd done nothing. Nor did he seem the kind of man to leave women to fend for themselves. There was no question in Avril's mind that he was a man of conscience, that she could trust him.

Now that she'd made that decision, she couldn't reach the cottage quickly enough.

When Avril left to milk the ewe, Brandr realized he didn't have much time. He began working on Kimbery at once.

"How would you like to play Fenrir, Kimmie?" he asked, licking his lips, hoping his ploy would work.

Kimbery played coy. "Maybe."

"You can be Fenrir. And I'll be Tyr, Fenrir's loyal friend."

The little girl hesitated, swaying indecisively for a moment. Then she dropped to all fours on the floor and began snapping her teeth together, pretending to be a ferocious wolf.

He spoke in the growling voice of Tyr. "You're so strong, Fenrir, stronger than any other god. I wonder if you're strong enough to break one of those sticks in two." He nodded to the kindling near the hearth.

Kimbery snarled and picked up a twig in her jaws, then took it out with her hands and broke it.

He gasped in feigned awe. "I wonder if you're strong

enough to pick up that sword and bring it here all by yourself."

Kimbery hesitated at that and sat back on her heels. "Mama said wee lasses aren't supposed to touch her sword."

Silently cursing in frustration, he said in Tyr's voice, "Wee lasses? But you're not a wee lass. You're Fenrir, son of Loki, son of Odin, the most powerful of all the gods."

The little girl roared once, but then she came close and whispered in his ear. "Mama doesn't even want Fenrir to touch her sword."

Brandr sighed. Avril had her trained well, that was certain. But it didn't matter. He could get free without the sword.

"Great Fenrir," he intoned, "I wonder if you're strong enough to escape this heavy collar."

Kimbery gave a fierce growl of agreement.

"I'll take it off my neck," he said, "and you can put it around yours." He made a show of trying to break free of the collar, twisting and straining.

She became Kimbery again for a moment, whispering, "I'll unbuckle it, and then you can put it on me."

"All right," he whispered back.

As her tiny fingers worked on the strap, a feeling of misgiving weighed down his heart. He didn't want to hurt the little girl. He didn't want to betray her mother. But he saw no other way. He couldn't endanger them. And he had to leave before Avril returned or she'd tempt him into staying.

The instant his neck was free, he bent forward to untie

the ropes about his wrists with his teeth.

"Put it on me!" Kimbery impatiently demanded.

"I can't until I loose my hands," he explained.

"Hurry."

He did. As soon as his wrists were free, he untied the rope around his middle, then moved aside so Kimbery could stand in his place.

He buckled the collar loosely around her neck so she wouldn't be able to follow him or hurt herself. She bared her teeth in a snarl as he struggled to his feet on legs that had grown weak with sitting.

While Kimbery growled and twisted against the collar, Brandr glanced at the jeweled sword.

In the end, he found he couldn't bring himself to take it. The blade was Avril's hard-won prize, a gift from her father, and her only defense.

He straightened slowly, groaning at the strain of his stiff muscles. Kimbery quieted. She was eyeing him uneasily now.

"You're Tyr," she said. "You're supposed to put your hand in my mouth."

He meant to leave without a word and without a backward glance. It was best if Kimbery remembered him as a bad man.

But his betrayal must have been written on his face. Kimmie's chin began to tremble. "Nay, Da. Don't go."

He gulped as a knot of emotion rose up to choke him. He wanted to kneel before her and take her in his arms one last time, to give her the farewell embrace he'd never been able to give his own daughter.

But he couldn't. He had to leave...now.

The words spilled out of him in a rush. "I have to, Kimmie. But I'll never forget you. I promise."

Then, before tears could engulf them both, he slipped out the cottage door, closing it behind him. He headed toward the sea, where Avril would never think to look for him.

Avril froze as she closed the pasture gate and noticed the distant figure limping along the shore. It took three heartbeats for her to recognize who it was and another two to realize the significance.

She dropped the bucket, and milk spilled across the ground.

Kimmie!

Fear sucked all the moisture out of her mouth as she hurtled toward the cottage.

When she threw open the door, she was relieved to find Kimbery relatively unhurt. Still, her hands shook as she rushed forward to unbuckle the collar around the little girl's neck.

"He left, Mama," Kimmie sobbed. "We were playing...and he left."

Avril wavered between humiliation and rage. How she'd been so gulled, she didn't know. But now she cursed her stupid trusting heart. She'd been right from the beginning. She should never have trusted a Viking.

"Make him come back, Mama," Kimbery pleaded as she wrapped her arms around Avril's neck, tears streaming down her face.

Avril's heart felt like a lump of lead. Brandr must have

tricked her the entire time, making her believe he was decent, gentle, civil. It made her sick to think she'd ever imagined he was in love with her. It made her even more nauseous to remember what she'd let him do to her.

She'd believed him. Kimbery had believed him. He'd pretended that he was different from the berserkers who'd come before, that he was noble and honorable. Yet he was no less a marauder, doing his damage and running off like a coward.

The brute had broken poor Kimbery's heart.

"I want Da!" Kimmie wailed.

Avril gave her a comforting squeeze as tears welled in her own eyes.

But as she held her weeping daughter and tried to soothe her own frayed emotions, it wasn't long before her hurt turned into anger and her anger into action.

Damn the Viking! Who did he think he was to steal away like a thief in the night? He owed her an explanation. He owed Kimbery an explanation. He'd been a father. He knew how sensitive children were. How dared he slink off out of Kimbery's life without so much as a word of farewell?

By God, one way or another, she'd make him answer to her.

She gently swept Kimmie's hair back from her sad little face and used her thumbs to wipe away the tears.

"Listen, Kimmie," she said, "I'm going to go after him. I need you to stay. Do you understand?"

She nodded.

But the moment Avril went for her sword, Kimmie panicked. "Nay, Mama, don't hurt him!"

She frowned. "I won't." At least, she *hoped* she wouldn't, though at the moment, the idea of running him through had its appeal.

"You promise?"

Avril didn't want to make a promise she couldn't keep, but she knew Kimbery would be unmanageable if she didn't. "I promise...if you promise not to set foot outside the cottage."

"I promise." Avril nodded in approval, and as she whirled to go, Kimmie added plaintively, "Bring him back home, Mama."

Home. This wasn't his home. But she couldn't deny, even after so few days, she too had begun to think of Brandr as part of her little family.

Without a word, she swept out the door and raced down to the water's edge to catch up with her quarry.

Brandr didn't realize he'd been followed until he felt something sharp jab him in the back.

"Hold it right there."

He froze. That was the point of her jeweled sword, no doubt. He knew he should have taken it. But how had she managed to find him? He was a good mile down the shore from her cottage.

Glancing down, he realized the waves rushing over the sand had only partially covered his footprints. They'd also completely covered the sound of her pursuit.

His shoulders sank. He'd hoped to avoid a confrontation. He'd hoped to escape quietly, letting Avril think he was a harmless coward like Loki—a knave who'd deserted her but wasn't worth hunting down.

"Where do you think you're going?" she demanded.

"Away."

"Without a word?" she asked, clearly vexed. "Without even saying goodbye?" She poked him with the sword, and he flinched. "How could you do that to...to a sweet little girl like Kimbery?"

Brandr could tell that Kimbery wasn't the only one hurt by his desertion. But he didn't dare let Avril know how he really felt. "She'll get over it."

His cold words hung on the air as a wave crashed on the rocks and hissed over the sand.

"Get over it?" she bit out. "You. Bloody. Bastard."

He clenched his jaw against a surge of guilt.

"She called you Da," she said.

He closed his eyes against the pain.

"Damn you, Viking," she muttered. "I would have set you free."

"I know."

Behind him, she gasped. "If you knew, then why did you sneak off like a robber? Kimbery trusted you." Her voice broke. "She...cared for you."

He furrowed his brow. He cared for Kimbery. She'd brought a welcome light back into his life, a light that had been extinguished when his own children had been taken from him. As for Avril... He was afraid his feelings for Avril went far beyond merely caring for her.

Clenching his fists, he spoke with a flippancy he didn't feel. "She's a child. She'll forget me."

He heard her sob, but she covered her hurt quickly with a jab of her sword that made him wince. "Why would you do such a hurtful thing? Why would you desert her?"

"It's for her own good," he growled.

"You son of a..." She suddenly gave his arse a punishing whack with the flat of her blade. He jerked and raised his hands in surrender. "What the hell is *that* supposed to mean?" she demanded. "You wash up on my beach, sleep under my roof, eat my food, befriend my daughter, and you suddenly decide to walk out of her life...for her own good?"

Brandr decided not to remind her that those were things over which he'd had no choice. After all, she was upset, and she had a sword in her hand. "It *is* for her own good. You said it yourself. I'm a bad man."

"You know that's not true."

"Isn't it?" It was best if she went on thinking he was a heartless brute. Leaving her would be twice as hard if she begged him to stay. "I'm a Viking, a marauder, an invader."

"She liked you. She...she loved you."

Brandr squeezed his eyes shut. He knew Avril was no longer talking about Kimbery now.

He could hear the hurt in her vexed murmur. "Damn you, did you care nothing for her? Was it all a ruse? How could you make her believe you had feelings for her and then...and then abandon her?"

Brandr didn't mean to respond. It would be better for everyone if he let it go. But the words spilled forth. "Do you think it was easy?" he choked out over his shoulder. "To walk away like that? To leave her, knowing she trusted me? Do you think it was easy abandoning her, knowing I was breaking her heart?"

"Why then?" she sobbed. "Why did you run away?"

"I had to."

"You're a coward," she said bitterly, "just like all the men I've known."

"Nay!" he insisted, unwilling to let her believe that. "The man who raped you was a coward. The man who killed your father was a coward. The men who stole your land were cowards."

"And you're not?"

"Nay! I'm trying to protect you."

"I can protect myself."

"Not from me."

"That makes no—"

"I'm cursed, Avril," he ground out. "I'm...cursed. Everyone I care about has been taken from me. My wife. My children. My village. My men." His throat closed, but he forced the words out. "I won't let that happen to Kimbery. And I won't let that happen to you."

For a moment, the only sound was the hushed whisper of the incoming tide and a single gull squawking softly overhead.

Then Avril responded with surprise to his confession. "You...care about me?"

He hung his head and sighed. Was it not written all over his face? He gave her a rueful chuckle. "Oh, my Pictish temptress," he said, shaking his head, "it's far worse than that. I fear I'm in love with you."

Avril was struck speechless. She lowered the blade

from his back as his words sank in. No one had ever said that to her before. She didn't know how to respond. She'd fantasized about being Brandr's wife, about making a family with him. She'd never imagined he might already have feelings for her.

She stared in wonder at the enemy she'd discovered only days before on this very shore. His long Viking-blond hair tangled over his wide invader's shoulders and fell down his broad marauding back. But though he was definitely still a stranger, he no longer seemed a foe.

Now she saw the possibility of a bright future...for Kimbery, for herself, for the shipwrecked Northman. They *could* make a life together. They *could* find a place in the world. All she had to do was persuade Brandr of that.

He glanced over his shoulder. Misunderstanding her silence and her lowered weapon, he asked somberly, "Will you let me go now?"

She whipped the point of her blade back up so swiftly it startled him. "Not so fast, Viking." A thrill of hope suffused her even as her eyes filled with happy tears. One way or another, she'd convince the Northman to stay...even if she had to keep him leashed in her cottage for a year. "I thought you said you weren't a coward."

He didn't answer.

She continued. "You're a damned Northman! You flex your muscle, rattle your battleaxe, and speak of glorious war. And yet you'd run away from a *curse*?"

He clenched his fists, but remained silent.

"Well," she said, "I don't believe in curses. Do you think you alone are fortune's foe? I've lost everything, too. I've had bad times when I wanted to surrender. I've had moments of weakness when I wondered why I went on living. But I never gave up. Not once did I let despair get the better of me. Not once did I—"

"Mama!" Kimbery called out suddenly behind her.

Avril started in surprise.

"Kimbery!" she snapped, whipping around to give her daughter the scolding of her life. "I told you to stay at..."

But when she saw Kimmie hadn't come alone, Avril's heart plummeted, her knees buckled, and she nearly lost her grip on the sword. Her little girl was riding merrily atop the shoulders of one of dozens of Viking savages that now occupied her beach.

"Look!" Kimbery crowed, oblivious to her horror. "I'm a Frost Giant!"

All of Avril's warrior instincts told her not to show weakness, not to waver, not to beg. Five years ago, standing over her father's grave, bruised from a brutal rape, she'd vowed never to cower before a Viking again.

But five years ago, she hadn't had a daughter she'd die for.

"Nay," she choked out, "please. Don't hurt her." She prayed they could understand her words. Oh, God, she thought, what if they meant to steal Kimbery? What if they sailed away with her to the North? What if Avril never saw her again?

Quaking with fear, she moved her sword away from Brandr and set the weapon gently on the ground. "Take him. Take Brandr. Just give my daughter back to me."

CHAPTER 11

Brandr wheeled around with his fists raised and his face in a fierce scowl, ready to fight whoever was threatening the women he loved. He lowered his arms immediately when he saw who it was.

"Halfdan?" he asked in disbelief. "Ragnarr?" Relief and joy coursed through him. Behind Avril stood his brothers—whole, healthy, and grinning. By the grace of Odin, they'd come through the storm, untouched, and they were surrounded by their men. "You're alive!"

There was a rumble of celebration as he rushed forward to catch his brothers in a one-armed embrace.

"What happened to you?" Ragnarr asked, indicating his splinted forearm.

His injury was the least of Brandr's concerns. "A scratch," he said with a shrug. "But how did you find me?"

Halfdan frowned. "We followed the wreckage of your ship."

Brandr nodded. There was a long moment of

reflective silence as everyone thought about those who'd been lost. Then Ragnarr cleared his throat and announced, "Your men are no doubt feasting in Valhalla."

There were cheers of agreement all around.

"But it's been days," Brandr said. "The wreckage must have drifted. How did you know to look for me here?"

Halfdan gave him a half-smile. "It might have something to do with the little girl standing in her cottage door, yelling 'Brandr! Brandr!' at the top of her lungs."

Brandr had to smile at that. Kimbery perched happily atop ferocious Axlan's shoulders as if he were her favorite uncle.

"So tell me," Ragnarr asked, crossing his arms and cocking a brow toward Avril, "how did my big warrior brother end up at the pointed end of a Pictish wench's sword?"

Brandr was so grateful to see his brothers that he didn't mind the taunt. There would be time to salvage his pride later. But when he looked back at Avril, he saw she'd gone white with fear. She didn't understand their language. She didn't know who they were or what they intended. And her gaze was fixed on Kimbery.

He switched back to Pictish. "Avril, it's all right. They won't hurt you."

Of course, he knew she had no reason to trust him. He'd manipulated her. He'd betrayed her. He'd abandoned her.

"Please, Brandr," she said almost inaudibly. "Please don't take her. Don't take Kimbery."

He furrowed his brows. He wouldn't dream of taking a

child from her mother. None of his men would. That she could even think him capable of such cruelty made him want to strangle the berserkers who'd so badly damaged her.

But as he looked at her, a spark of desperate courage flashed in her eyes, and before he could see what she intended, she dove for her blade. In an instant, she swept up the weapon and trained the point at his throat.

"Put her down!" she yelled at the men. "Put her down right now!"

"Nay!" Kimmie wailed in protest.

"Put her down, or I'll cut his throat!"

Brandr froze. He probably could have knocked aside the sword with a swing of his splinted arm, but it was risky. He knew better than to come between a mother and her child.

"Avril," he said, "they mean her no—"

"Quiet!" she barked.

"Woman," Halfdan said in broken Pictish, "you are one. We are many. Put down your sword."

Avril was trembling, but her blade didn't waver an inch. "Nay."

Ragnarr frowned. "Nay?"

"Nay," she said. "Put her down, or I'll kill him."

Brandr tensed as several of the men clapped hands on their weapons in challenge.

"I mean it," she bit out. "Put her down, get back on your ship, and sail away from here, or I swear I'll cut his throat."

Most of the men figured she was bluffing. Maidens

didn't kill people, especially Northmen who were double their size. Unintimidated by her threat, Halfdan drew his sword. And when Ragnarr unfolded his arms, he was holding twin axes. Disaster loomed. Brandr had to temper things before the tense standoff erupted into an ugly battle.

"Wait!" he shouted. Avril might believe she had leverage, but Brandr had seen his brothers and their men at war. No one opposed them and lived. It was up to him to prevent a violent altercation. "Don't hurt her!"

"Don't hurt her?" Halfdan echoed in amazement. "If you hadn't noticed, *she's* the one holding a blade to *your* throat."

"She won't do it," Brandr said, hoping he was right. "She won't kill me."

"That's right," Ragnarr said, "because *we'll* kill *her* before she gets the chance."

"Nay! She...she saved my life." It wasn't exactly true, but he didn't know what would have happened to him if she hadn't dragged him into her cottage. Probably her neighbor would have found him, killed him, and made a trophy out of him.

"Saved your life?" Halfdan scoffed. "She doesn't seem too interested in your life now."

Brandr sighed. Halfdan was right, of course. But if they'd shown up an hour earlier, it would have been a different tale. He would have told them how she'd set his arm, kept him fed, and protected him from a Viking-hunter. And he would have been able to explain to Avril that his brothers meant her no harm, that *he* meant her no harm.

Now, he could hardly expect her to trust him.

But maybe, now that his brothers were here, now that he was no longer shipwrecked and alone, now that he had a small army at his disposal...

A brilliant idea took form in his mind, and for the first time in a year, he began to think he might not be cursed after all.

To commit to slaying Brandr if it came to that was the most difficult thing Avril had ever done in her life. But her precious daughter was at risk. Nothing was more important than Kimbery—nothing.

"Avril," Brandr said, "listen to me. You know you don't want to kill me in cold blood. It's not the honorable thing to do. And you always do the honorable thing."

She clamped her lips together. But though her vision grew watery and a tense knot formed in her throat at what she might be forced to do, she held her ground. She realized that when it came to her daughter, Kimbery was more important than honor itself.

"Make them put her down," she said hoarsely, "or I swear I'll slay you where you stand."

He seemed to believe her. "All right." He said something to his men. They argued back and forth. But in the end, they put away their weapons, muttering in disgust as they did so.

"And Kimmie," she choked out. "Give me my daughter."

"Nay!" Kimmie complained. The wayward little sprite tucked her lip under her teeth and held tightly to the man's head. Kimbery knew she was in trouble for

disobeying Avril's orders and didn't want to be punished.

But punishment was the last thing on Avril's mind. All she wanted was to get Kimbery back, safe and sound.

"I didn't set foot outside the cottage, Mama," Kimmie said. "I didn't. The Frost Giants picked me up."

"Brandr," Avril demanded, willing her voice to remain steady, "make them put her down."

He relayed her message. Despite Kimmie's protests, the man peeled the little girl's hands from his forehead and lifted her off of his shoulders.

"Come here, Kimmie," Avril said, her heart in her throat.

Kimbery reluctantly began to saunter over, and for one tiny instant, Avril lost her focus. But in that instant and without warning, Brandr used his arm—the arm Avril had splinted for him—and knocked her sword aside, and then used his good hand to wrench it from her grasp. She was still gasping in dismay when he wrapped his splinted arm around her neck, trapping her against him.

She clawed and kicked at him, but nothing would dislodge the brute's grip on her. In desperation, she cried, "Run, Kimmie! Run!"

Kimbery might be a willful little girl, but she recognized the alarm in Avril's voice. Obedient for once, she spun and began tearing across the sand toward home. The men casually watched her go.

Brandr blew out an annoyed breath. "All right," he said, "we're all going back to the cottage. Avril, you and I are going to have an *althing*. Do you remember what that is?"

She wasn't interested in conversing with him. All she cared about was keeping the men away from Kimbery. She twisted violently in his grip.

He ignored her struggles. "You and I are going to talk things over," he explained. "Together. Civilly."

With unflappable calm, he began to haul her, kicking and screaming, along the shore and back to the cottage, with his men in tow. By the time they arrived, she was hoarse and exhausted, but at least she had the satisfaction of knowing she'd put up a fight. She'd been no victim this time. She'd done everything she could to protect herself and her daughter.

"Kimmie!" Brandr called.

"Nay!" Avril yelled.

"Kimmie, come out!"

Kimbery popped her head out of the door.

"Nay!" Avril shrieked. "Stay there."

"She'll come to no harm, I promise," Brandr told her. "The men will watch over her."

He spoke as if she had a choice. The truth was she was at their mercy. Yet, when she thought about it, Brandr's men had done Kimmie no harm thus far. They could have kidnapped her when they first discovered her. They could have leveraged her life for Brandr's. But they hadn't.

She swallowed hard. "If they lay a finger on her..."

"They won't. I swear it. She'll be safe." One side of his mouth curved up. "She likes them. She thinks they're Frost Giants."

His smile of encouragement did little to assuage her

fears. And to her dismay, Kimbery ran eagerly toward the man who'd hefted her on his shoulders, wrapping her arms fondly around his knees. With an uneasy spirit and against her better judgment, Avril let Brandr steer her into the cottage.

The instant he closed the door behind them, he let her go. She staggered a step and wheeled on him, ready to fight with her bare hands, if need be.

"Sheathe your claws, kitten," he said. "I only want to talk."

She scowled at him, and then, realizing her fists were no match for a sword, lowered her hands.

"I have an idea," he told her, beginning to pace pensively before the hearth.

She touched her scraped throat, rubbed raw from struggling against his splinted arm. "An idea." She couldn't imagine what he meant.

"My brothers and I came to your land, not to invade, but to settle," he said, gesturing with her sword. "All we want is a place to stay. A home. Land."

She scowled, only half-listening, wondering if there was any way she could wrest her sword from his grip. She ground out, "I don't think you'll all fit in my cottage, if that's your idea."

He gave her an indulgent chuckle, and then continued. "Nay, I have a far better plan." He stopped pacing and arched a brow at her. "How far away is Rivenloch?"

She blinked. "Rivenloch?" What was he thinking?

He smiled at her. It was wicked smile, a scheming smile.

She opened her mouth to speak and then closed it again, once, twice. Could he possibly be considering what she *thought* he was considering?

"I have an army of Northmen," he said. "Enough to take back a castle wrongfully seized from its true heir."

For a moment, she was stunned. But as she looked into his glittering blue eyes, a thrill of hope shot through her. "Are you serious?"

"I am." His face was grim now, and he suddenly looked every inch a coldhearted, bloodthirsty Viking. "Are you?"

Avril stared at him in wide-eyed wonder. Mere moments ago, she'd been sure her life was over. Now it seemed full of promise beyond her wildest dreams.

Brandr flipped her sword over in his hand and offered it to her, jeweled hilt first. She stared down at it, knowing the final decision was in her hands. He wasn't just offering her a weapon. He was offering her his sword arm. He was offering her the might of his men. He was offering her her legacy.

Unable to find words to convey her gratitude, she silently took the sword from him. As she gazed down at the glowing gems of the hilt, they winked up at her, as if eager for battle. But after a moment, she propped the weapon against the wall.

There would be time to make war later.

Now, she wanted to make love.

CHAPTER 12

Brandr knew Avril would be pleased with his offer. He didn't realize just how pleased. Nor did he anticipate how she'd choose to express her pleasure...until she nudged him backward through the doorway of her bedchamber, covering his face with eager kisses.

He shivered as she ran her hands under his shirt and over his chest, and then gasped in pleased surprise as she shoved him back onto the bed. She climbed atop him, lifting his shirt to press her warm lips to his bare flesh. These Pictish women were uncommonly aggressive, he decided. But he definitely could get used to that.

He smiled as she hooked her arm possessively around his neck and claimed his mouth with hers. But his smile fell away as her other hand ventured boldly beneath the waist of his trousers.

Caught off-guard, he sucked in a quick breath as the blood surged through him. Overcome by an unexpected

rush of desire, he squeezed his eyes shut, hardening with astonishing speed at her touch.

She purred with satisfaction as her fingers curved naturally around his firm length, and he echoed the sound with a lusty growl. She slanted her mouth over his, plunging her tongue between his lips, and he instinctively reached up to clasp her face between his hands, deepening the kiss.

Her fingers scrabbled at the ties of his trousers, and he lifted his hips so she could slide them down.

With almost frantic haste, she raised her skirts and positioned herself to take him inside her.

His lust-starved body wanted her. Now. But everything was happening too fast. Though he'd imagined making love to her countless times in the past few days, it had never been like this. He had no time to seduce her, no chance to learn her body—to feast his eyes upon her breasts, to whisper in her ear, to kiss the strange design on her shoulder, to suck gently at her nipples, to part her thighs and fondle the sweet bud that guarded her womanhood.

It was too late to stop now. She seized his wrists and anchored his arms to the bed, forcefully sinking down upon him until he was sheathed to the hilt.

He groaned with pleasure as she had her way with him, riding him like a steed, grinding against his hips with a demanding rhythm that pushed him with reckless speed to the brink of passion.

If it hadn't been such a long time, if she hadn't caught him unawares, if he hadn't been so utterly swept away by his own needs, he would have forced her to slow down. But like a boy trysting for the first time, he was beyond reason and out of control.

Almost before he could draw another breath, the blood began to simmer in his veins. A flash like hot lightning seared his skin. The tide of desire rose in him, raging like a flood, filling him with need, and then bursting free in a quenching rush.

With a bellow of ecstasy, he arched up into her welcoming womb, pulsing out waves of molten fire. He heard her sigh in response, and when he was able to gaze at her from beneath his heavy lids, Brandr glimpsed intoxicating triumph on her face.

He shuddered with the power of his release while she replied with a throaty, pleased chuckle. And then, unable to formulate coherent thoughts, much less words, he simply lay beneath her, panting like a winded warhorse.

While he caught his breath, she lazily ran her fingers over the bulge of his upper arm. She bit her lower lip, flushed with longing, and he could see unrequited desire still veiling her eyes.

He wasn't finished with her. This hasty coupling had been far too swift and one-sided. But it had taken the ragged edge off of his lust, and now he'd be able to take his time with the hot-blooded wench.

Avril knew everything was going to be all right now. She'd won Brandr over, body and soul. He'd marry her now and give Kimbery a name. He'd even promised to regain Rivenloch and her rightful place of power. There was nothing as heady as being in control again. At last her world would be set to rights and she'd get her command back.

And yet she realized as she continued to gaze down at Brandr's broad chest, tracing the contours of his muscular arms and shivering at the rasp of his breath upon her skin, she felt less like the lady and commander of a castle and more like a drowsy-eyed cat longing to be pet.

The feeling troubled her. Her heart beat too fast. Her reflexes were too slow. She felt feverish and weak, as if her bones were melting. And the sensation only grew worse when she felt him begin to swell inside her again.

She knew she should withdraw. She was too exposed, too fragile, too vulnerable. If she wasn't careful, she'd leave herself open to attack. She might find herself at his mercy, the same way she'd been at the mercy of that berserker.

And yet...

She couldn't seem to pull away. Even as her mind screamed at her to flee while she still had the chance, to raise her shield, to guard her heart, as she gazed into his smoldering eyes and felt the impassioned rise and fall of his formidable chest, she was strangely drawn to him.

And when one corner of his mouth lifted in a lazy smile, when he reached up to softly brush her lower lip with the back of his knuckle, when she felt the subtle pulse of his need within her, she knew she was past escape.

Her eyes closed, and her mouth fell open beneath his touch. A curious warm glow enfolded her, softening her fear and whetting her appetite. Her fingers tightened on his shoulders, pressing into his supple flesh, as he gently caressed her cheek.

Her breath quickened as his fingers drifted down her throat, settling upon the place where her pulse now raced. She swallowed hard, knowing he could strangle her with one hand and yet trusting he would not.

Indeed, his hand moved with such sweet leisure down her neck, sweeping across her collar bone, and slipping beneath her kirtle, that she felt no desire to resist. Slowly, he teased the garment from her shoulder, running his fingers over the design inked there.

"What is this?" he whispered.

She furrowed her brow, startled that he spoke to her. The men she'd bedded before never uttered a word—not that she'd given them the chance. She hadn't wanted to know their thoughts. She'd simply wanted to use their bodies and be done with them.

It was disconcerting. Nonetheless, she managed to answer him. "An endless knot."

"It's beautiful," he murmured. "What does it mean?"

She hesitated, uncomfortable with his question. Somehow, the exchange of words made what they did more intimate. She couldn't pretend he was just another body. Speaking forced her to acknowledge he was a man...with thoughts and ideas and intentions.

Though it was difficult for her, she answered him in a stilted whisper. "The three circles are...spirit...life...and love."

"Ah." His hand left her shoulder then to brush over her

ankle, which was nestled against his hip. "And this one?"

Lusty lethargy made her voice ragged and foreign to her ears. "A broken sword...in honor of my father."

He was silent for a moment. Then he asked, "Did it hurt?"

His puzzling question made her open her eyes. Then she remembered he had no such markings on his skin. Her designs must seem strange to him.

"Nay," she told him.

He shot her a dubious glance.

"A wee bit," she admitted.

He grinned at her again, and the fond shimmer in his eyes made her return his smile. Suddenly she felt more than just the sharp heat of lust and longing. There was also a gentle warmth like that of a banked fire. And as he continued to hold her gaze, she sensed he could easily stir the coals of that fire to life.

His eyes lowered to her mouth, and already she longed to taste him again. As if drawn to him by the force of his will, she closed her eyes and leaned toward him.

This time she made no demands of him, but let him lead. His kiss was tender and tentative, like the touch of a honeybee upon a blossom, and soon a pleasant buzzing filled her head. Again and again he sampled the nectar from her lips, until she ached for more.

As she gasped against his mouth, he deftly loosened the laces of her kirtle and slipped it from her shoulders. When it caught on the points of her breasts, he freed it, sliding one fingertip under the linen. When his knuckle grazed her nipple, desire welled in her like the swelling of an ocean wave, submerging her in its powerful current.

She clenched her thighs around his hips and moved against him. But he refused to engage her yet, focusing instead on her bared bosom. He kissed his way down her throat and across her breast, pausing as he reached the inch-long strip of puckered flesh there.

"Your battle scar?" he murmured.

She nodded, and he traced its length with his tongue before blazing a searing trail toward her nipple. When he sucked softly there, she cried out in wonder at the divine sensation.

Then, just when she thought she would burst from pleasure, he moved to her other breast, lavishing it with equal attention. Moans issued from her throat unbidden, and her fingers tangled in his hair as if to keep him close.

While she reveled in a languorous haze, his hand delved beneath her skirts, traveling up her thigh with silky stealth. Even knowing where he was headed couldn't prepare her for the shock that rocked her when the tip of his finger touched her at the spot where their bodies joined.

He rubbed gently there, and she squeezed her eyes shut, caught in a paralyzing tide of euphoria. She arched against him, elated yet languishing, knowing she wanted something more, something she could neither define nor understand.

This was far more potent than the intoxication of his surrender. It was a savage craving that satiated and

tormented her all at once. Lost in a fog of emotions, she was nonetheless compelled to sail onward.

It was only when his arm wrapped around her shoulders and his thigh curved possessively over her buttock, when he tried to roll her onto her back, that she stiffened.

Only once had a man ever dominated her. And that had been against her will. After she'd been raped, she'd never allowed a man to toss her onto her back. She'd been helpless once. She'd vowed never to be so again.

"Nay!" She dug her nails into his shoulders, ready to resist with all her might.

To her surprise, he responded immediately, relaxing his grip on her and withdrawing his hands. She searched his face, wondering what game he played.

But there was only patient affection in his eyes. And as he lay submissively beneath her, giving her time to reason, she was forced to confront her demons. It wasn't long before she realized the truth—those demons clearly existed only in her imagination.

Brandr was not a berserker. He had no desire to hurt her, to demean her, to dominate her. He obviously cared for her. He'd confessed his love. He'd bared his soul to her. Hell, he'd even offered to fight for her. Why, then, was she reluctant to cede the tiniest bit of control to him?

If anyone was obsessed with power, Avril realized, it was she. After all, she'd held him prisoner. She'd kept him at her mercy. She'd had her way with him. What more did she want? Must he grovel at her feet, yielding to her in every way?

At her brooding silence, he smiled ruefully. "Maybe you don't truly care for me."

She frowned. How could he think that? She'd practically saved his life. She'd fed him and housed him. She'd set his arm. She'd protected him from her neighbor. How could she not care for the man who had promised to get her castle back? "Of course I do."

"But do you trust me?"

She bit her lip. It was true she'd learned to be wary when it came to trusting men. And yet Brandr had done nothing to deserve her mistrust. Even when she thought he'd betrayed her, he'd only been trying to protect her. She looked into his expectant eyes—eyes as beautiful and unclouded as a summer sky—and then lowered her gaze to his inviting mouth.

She couldn't let the damned berserker who'd raped her win. She couldn't let her wretched brothers win. She wouldn't let what had happened to her in the past ruin her chances at happiness in the future.

"Kiss me again," she murmured, certain that she *did* trust him after all.

His touch was tender and coaxing, soothing and arousing all at once. He cradled her chin and kissed her with care, as if she were a brittle seashell. He stroked her hair with the gentle caress of the ocean combing the kelp. His fingers swept over her like the incoming tide washing across the shore, exploring higher and farther with subtle stealth.

And this time, when she willingly rolled onto her back, it felt as natural as turning over in the sea on an afternoon swim. And though he rose above her, as massive and menacing as an ocean wave, she felt no panic. He moved with the steady languor of the sea, rocking her gently along the current until they floated there together in rising bliss.

Before long, she realized this was like no other voyage she'd taken. The sensual weight of his hips, the tantalizing touch of his hands, the fiery caress of his tongue took her to a place she'd never been before. Her breath expanded as an ember sparked within her, filling her with glowing heat. Her body moved of its own accord, squirming in pleasure. Her fingers pressed into the supple muscle of his buttocks, urging him closer, and when that wasn't enough, she wrapped her legs around him, arching up against the divine pressure of his belly. She closed her eyes tightly, relishing the erotic delight of his flesh on hers as he teased her lust to a fine point.

Farther and farther into uncharted waters they sailed, and Avril clung to him, half-afraid, half-obsessed, seeking...seeking...

"Look at me," he suddenly breathed.

She couldn't. She'd never felt so vulnerable, so exposed. If she let him glimpse the helplessness in her eyes...

"Look at me," he softly urged, pausing to smooth away the crease between her brows with his thumb.

With a small whimper of protest, she reluctantly complied, and her face grew instantly hot with shame. But then she gazed into his eyes—his shining, smoldering, sea-colored eyes.

As he stared down at her with pure, beautiful,

unflinching love, her fears vanished. A sweetness filled her spirit, softening her, comforting her. And when he moved within her again, the tenderness between them heightened her desire.

She sailed with him on the journey toward passion, and the lovely torment in his eyes fueled her own as they grew closer and closer to the edge of the world...panting, gasping, then breathless with intensity as time froze and the earth dropped from below. Lightning struck her with stunning force, making her cry out in shock, while Brandr echoed her with a low groan.

Their shudders of release made powerful thunder, and she held tightly to him as they careened earthward again, falling...falling...back into the deep calm of the sea.

For a long while she drifted on the lazy current, miles away from care, letting waves of contentment wash over her.

Gradually, the fog of sensuality receded, and she began to notice small details like the skirt rucked up indecently around her waist, the adorable lock of hair drooping over his forehead, the rock-hard object stabbing into her spine...

With a frown, she reached behind her back and dug out Kimbery's slate and a piece of charcoal.

He lifted his head and grinned at the smeared slate. "You may have a new design on your back."

She smiled back. "I suspect it may be a drawing of you." She tossed the slate and charcoal aside and reached up to touch that irresistible blond lock. "You know, I think I could get used to these *althings* of yours."

147

He turned her hand to kiss her palm. "Strange, but I don't remember them ever being so...invigorating."

She lowered her gaze to his delectable mouth, and he accepted her unspoken invitation at once. They were mid-kiss when there was a loud banging on the cottage door.

Avril gasped and yanked her kirtle up to her chin.

Brandr muttered, "My brothers no doubt fear you've thrust me through with your sword." With a last light kiss upon her brow, he rose from the bed and pulled up his trousers.

As she worked hastily to repair her appearance, he retrieved Kimbery's slate and drew a few strange runes on it with the charcoal.

"What does it say?" she asked.

He gave her a sweet, lopsided smile full of affection and mischief. "Da."

Her eyes welled with joy and gratitude as she took his hand and tugged him toward the door. She couldn't wait to tell Kimbery she'd been right all along.

Rivenloch was returned to its rightful heir. And in that place, generations of Vikings and Picts intermingled and intermarried to create the sturdy stock of Scotland. The descendants of Brandr and Avril upheld the honor in which their clan was forged. Their veins flowed with the courage and loyalty of their Viking father and their Pictish mother. For centuries, they bravely defended the land from invaders with an unconquerable army, an army made

strong by the marriage of their two powerful and illustrious cultures.

But one day, their courage and loyalty would be tested, for there would come to Rivenloch an enemy so formidable it would take warriors of unmatched mettle to face the daunting challenge.

These warriors would be the progeny of a centuries old Viking invader and his Pictish bride, and the fate of the clan would lie in their unlikely hands. Thus was born the legend of the Warrior Maids of Rivenloch...

The End

THANK YOU FOR READING MY BOOK!

Did you enjoy it? If so, I hope you'll post a review to let others know! There's no greater gift you can give an author than spreading your love of her books.

It's truly a pleasure and a privilege to be able to share my stories with you. Knowing that my words have made you laugh, sigh, or touched a secret place in your heart is what keeps the wind beneath my wings. I hope you enjoyed our brief journey together, and may ALL of your adventures have happy endings!

If you'd like to keep in touch, feel free to sign up for my monthly e-newsletter at www.glynnis.net, and you'll be the first to find out about my new releases, special discounts, prizes, promotions, and more!

If you want to keep up with my daily escapades:
Friend me at facebook.com/GlynnisCampbell
Like my Page at bit.ly/GlynnisCampbellFBPage
Follow me at twitter.com/GlynnisCampbell
And if you're a super fan, join
facebook.com/GCReadersClan

Laꝺy Danger

The Warrior Maids of Rivenloch Book 1

The Borders, Scotland
Summer 1136

"So. Where is the *third* wench?" Sir Pagan murmured casually, feeling *far* from casual as he and Colin du Lac hunkered behind the concealing cloud of heather, spying upon the two splendid maids bathing in the pond below.

Colin almost strangled on his incredulity. "God's breath, you greedy sot," he hissed. "Isn't it enough you have your choice of the pair of beauties yonder? Most men would give their sword arm to—"

Both men froze as the blonde woman, gloriously drenched in sunlight, sluiced water up over a creamy shoulder, rising above the waves enough to bare a pair of perfect breasts.

The blood drained from Pagan's face and rushed to his loins, making them ache fiercely. Lord, he should have swived that lusty harlot in the last town before he came to negotiate such matters. This was as foolish as shopping for provender with a full purse and an empty gut.

But somehow he managed an indifferent grunt, despite the overwhelming desire disrupting his thoughts and transfiguring his body. "A man never purchases a blade, Colin," he said hoarsely, "without inspecting all the swords in the shop."

"True, but a man never runs his thumb along the edge of a sword presented him by the *King*."

Colin had a point. Who was Sir Pagan Cameliard to question a gift from King David? Besides, it wasn't a weapon he chose. It was only a wife. "Pah." He swatted an irritating sprig of heather out of his face. "One woman is much the same as another, I suppose," he grumbled. "'Tis no matter which of them I claim."

Colin snorted in derision. "So say you *now*," he whispered, fixing a lustful gaze upon the bathers, "now that you've laid eyes on the bountiful selection." A low whistle shivered from between his lips as the more buxom of the two maids dove beneath the glittering waves, giving them a glimpse of bare, sleek, enticing buttocks. "Lucky bastard."

Pagan *did* consider himself lucky.

When King David first offered him a Scots holding and a wife to go with it, he'd half expected to find a crumbling keep with a withered old crone in the tower. One glance at the imposing walls of Rivenloch eased his fears on the first count. And to his astonishment, the prospective brides before him, delectable pastries the King had placed upon his platter, were truly the most appetizing he'd seen in a long while, perhaps *ever*. His stirring loins offered proof of that.

Still, the idea of marriage unnerved Pagan like a cat rubbed tail to whiskers.

"God's eyes, I can't decide which I'd rather swive," Colin mused, "that beauty with the sun-bleached locks or the curvy one with the wild tresses and enormous..." He released a shuddering sigh.

"Neither," Pagan muttered.

"Both," Colin decided.

Deirdre of Rivenloch tossed her long blonde hair over one shoulder. She could feel the intruders' eyes upon her, had felt them for some time.

It wasn't that she cared if she was caught at her bath. The sisters suffered from neither modesty nor shame. How could one be ashamed or proud of having what *every* woman possessed? If a stray lad happened to look upon them with misplaced lust, it was no more than folly on his part.

Deirdre ran her fingers through her wet tresses and cast another surreptitious glance up the hill, toward the thick heather and drooping willows. The eyes trained upon her now were likely just that, belonging to a couple of curious youths who'd never seen a naked maid before. But she didn't dare mention their presence to Helena, for her impetuous sister would likely draw her sword first and ask their business afterward. Nay, Deirdre would deal with their mischief later herself.

For now she had a grave matter to discuss with Helena. And not much time.

"You delayed Miriel?" she asked, running a palm full of sheep tallow soap along her forearm.

"I hid her *sais*," Helena confided, "and then told her I'd seen the stable lad skulking about her chamber earlier."

Deirdre nodded. That would keep their youngest sister busy for a while. Miriel allowed no one to touch her precious weapons from the Orient.

"Listen, Deir," Helena warned, "I won't let Miriel sacrifice herself. I don't care what Father says. She's too young to wed. Too young and too..." She sighed in exasperation.

"I know."

What they both left unspoken was the fact that their youngest sister wasn't forged of the same metal they were. Deirdre and Helena were their father's daughters. His Viking blood pumped through their hearts. Tall and strong, they possessed wills of iron and skills to match. Known throughout the Borders as the Warrior Maids of Rivenloch, they'd taken to the sword like a babe to the breast. Their father had raised them to be fighters, to fear no man.

Miriel, however, to the lord's dismay, had proved as delicate and docile as their long departed mother. Whatever warrior spirit might have been nurtured in her had been quelled by Lady Edwina, who'd begged that Miriel be spared what she termed the perversion of the other two sisters.

After their mother died, Miriel had tried to please their father in her own way, amassing an impressive collection of exotic weapons from traveling merchants, but she'd developed neither the desire nor the strength to wield them. She'd become, in short, the meek, mild, obedient daughter their mother desired. And so Deirdre and Helena had protected Miriel all her life from her own helplessness and their father's disappointment in her.

Now it was up to them to save her from an undesirable marriage.

Deirdre passed her sister the lump of soap. "Trust me, I have no intention of leading the lamb to slaughter."

The spark of battle flared in Helena's eyes. "We'll challenge this Norman bridegroom then?"

Deirdre frowned. She knew that not every conflict was best resolved on the battlefield, even if her sister did not. She shook her head.

Helena cursed under her breath and gave the water a disappointed slap. "Why not?"

"To defy the Norman is to defy the King."

Hel arched a brow in challenge. "And?"

Deirdre's frown deepened. One day Helena's audaciousness would be her undoing. "'Tis *treason*, Hel."

Helena puffed out an irritated breath and scrubbed at her arm. "'Tis hardly treason when we've been betrayed by our own King. This meddler is a Norman, Deirdre...a *Norman*." She sneered the word as if it were a disease. "Pah! I've heard they're so soft they can't grow a proper beard. And some say they bathe even their hounds in lavender." She shuddered with distaste.

Deirdre had to agree with her sister's frustration, if not her claims. Indeed, she'd been just as outraged upon learning that King David had handed over Rivenloch's stewardship, not to a Scot, but to one of his Norman allies. Aye, the man was reported to be a fierce warrior, but certainly he knew nothing about Scotland.

What complicated matters was that their father had launched no protest. But then the Lord of Rivenloch hadn't been right in his mind for months now. Deirdre frequently found him conversing with the air, addressing their dead mother, and he was ever losing his way in the keep. He seemed to live in some idyllic time in the past, where his rule was unquestioned and his lands secure.

But with the crown resting uneasily on Stephen's head, greedy English barons had begun to wreak havoc along the Borders, seizing what lands they could in the ensuing chaos.

So for the past year the sisters had hidden their father's infirmity as best they could, to maintain the illusion of power and to prevent the perception of Rivenloch as an easy target. Deirdre had served as steward of the holding and captain of the guard, with Helena as second in command, and Miriel had overseen the household and the accounts.

They'd managed adequately. But Deirdre was wise enough to know such subterfuge couldn't last forever. Maybe that was the reason for this sudden appointment by the King. Maybe rumors of their father's debility had spread.

So Deirdre had thought long on the matter and finally come to grips with the truth. While Rivenloch's knights were brave and capable, they hadn't fought a real battle since before she was born. Now, land-hungry warmongers threatened the Borders. Only a fortnight ago, a rogue English baron had brazenly attacked the Scots keep at Mirkloan, not fifty miles distant. Indeed, it might serve Rivenloch well to have the counsel of a warrior seasoned in combat, someone who could advise her in her command.

But the missive that had arrived last week bearing King David's seal, the one Deirdre had shared only with Helena, also commanded the hand of one of the Rivenloch daughters in marriage to the steward. Clearly, the King intended a more permanent position for the Norman knight.

The news had hit her like a mace in the belly. With the responsibility of managing the castle, the furthest thing from any of the sisters' minds had been marriage. That the King would wed one of them to a...foreigner...was inconceivable. Did David doubt Rivenloch's loyalty? Deirdre could only pray this compulsory marriage was his attempt to keep the holding at least half in her clan's hands.

She wanted to believe that, needed to believe it. Otherwise, she might be tempted to sweep up her own blade and join her hotheaded sister in a Norman massacre.

Helena had ducked under the water, cooling her wrath. Now she sprang up suddenly, sputtering and shaking her head like a hound, spraying drops everywhere. "I know! What if we waylay this Norman bridegroom in the wood?" she said eagerly. "Catch him off guard. Slice him to ribbons. Blame his death on The Shadow?"

For a moment, Deirdre could only stare mutely at her bloodthirsty little sister, whom she feared might be serious. "You'd slay a man unawares and accuse a common thief of his murder?" She scowled and grabbed the soap back. "Father named you rightly, Hel, for 'tis surely where you're bound. Nay," she decided, "no one is going to be killed. One of us will marry him."

"Why should we have to marry him?" Hel said with a pout. "Is it not loathsome enough we must surrender our keep to the whoreson?"

Deirdre clutched her sister's arm, demanding her gaze. "We'll surrender nothing. Besides, you know if one of *us* doesn't wed him, Miriel will offer herself up, whether we will it or not. And Father *will* let her do it. We can't allow that to happen."

Deirdre stared solemnly into her sister's eyes, and they exchanged the look of unspoken agreement they'd shared since they were young lasses, the look that said they'd do whatever it took to protect helpless Miriel.

Helena bit out a resigned curse, then muttered, "Stupid Norman. He doesn't even have a proper name. Who would christen a child Pagan?"

Deirdre didn't bother to remind her sister that *she* answered to the name of Hel. Even Deirdre had to agree, however, that Pagan was not a name that conjured up visions of responsible leadership. Or honor. Or mercy. Indeed, it sounded like the name of a barbaric savage.

Helena sighed heavily, then nodded and took the soap again. "'Twill be me then. I will wed this son of a whelp."

But Deirdre could see by the murderous gleam in

Hel's eyes that if she had her way, her new husband wouldn't survive the wedding night. And while Deirdre might not mourn the demise of the uninvited Norman, she had no wish to see her sister drawn and quartered by the King for his murder. "Nay," she said. "'Tis *my* burden. I'll marry him."

"Don't be a fool," Hel shot back. "I'm more expendable than you. Besides," she said with a scheming grin, rubbing the sheep tallow soap back and forth between her hands, "while I lull the bastard into complacency, you can marshal forces for a surprise attack. We'll win Rivenloch back from him, Deirdre."

"Are you mad?" Deirdre flicked water at her reckless sister. She had little patience for Helena's blind bravado. Sometimes Hel boasted like a Highlander, thinking all England could be conquered with but a dozen brawny Scots. "'Tis *King David's* will to marry off this Norman to one of us. What will you do when *his* army comes?"

Hel silently pondered her words.

"Nay," Deirdre said before Hel could come up with another rash plan. "*I* will wed the bast-...Norman," she corrected.

Helena sulked for a moment, then tried another tactic, asking slyly, "What if he prefers me? After all, I have more of what a man favors." She rose from the water, posturing provocatively to lend proof to her words. "I'm younger. My legs are more shapely. My breasts are bigger."

"Your mouth is bigger," Deirdre countered, unaffected by Hel's attempt at goading her. "No man likes a woman with a shrewish tongue."

Hel frowned. Then her eyes lit up again. "All right then. I'll fight you for him."

"Fight me?"

"The winner weds the Norman."

Deirdre bit her lip, seriously considering the challenge. Her odds of besting Hel were good, since she fought with far more control than her quick-tempered sister. And Deirdre was impatient enough with Hel's foolishness to take her up on her offer at once and see the matter settled. Almost.

But there were still the spies on the hill to deal with. And unless she was mistaken, that was Miriel hastening across the meadow toward them.

"Hush!" Deirdre hissed. "Miriel comes. We'll speak no more of this." Deirdre squeezed the water from her hair. "The Normans should arrive in a day or two. I'll make my decision by nightfall. In the meantime, keep Miriel here. I have something to attend to."

"The men on the hill?"

Deirdre blinked. "You know?"

Hel lifted a sardonic brow. "How could I not? The sound of their drool hitting the sod would wake the dead. You're sure you don't need assistance?"

"There can't be more than two or three."

"Two. And they're highly distracted."

"Good. Keep them that way."

"God be praised," Colin said under his breath, "here comes the third." He nodded toward the delicate, dark-haired figure scampering across the grassy field sloping down to the pond, disrobing as she came. "Lord, she's a pretty one, sweet and small, like a succulent little cherry."

Pagan had suspected the last sister might be missing a limb or several teeth or most of her wits. But though she looked frail and less imposing than her curvaceous sisters, she, too, possessed a body to shame a goddess. He could only shake his head in wonder.

"Sweet Mary, Pagan," Colin said with a sigh as the third maid jumped into the pond, and they began splashing about like disporting sirens. "Whose arse did you kiss? The King's himself?"

Pagan frowned, bending a stem of heather between his fingers. What *had* he done to deserve his pick of these beauties? Aye, he'd served David in battle several times, but he'd met the King in Scotland only once, at Moray. David had seemed to like him well enough, and Pagan *had* saved a number of the King's men from walking into a rebel ambush that day. But surely that was no more than any commander would have done.

"Why would David hand over such a prize?" he pondered aloud. "And why to me?"

Colin snickered in amusement. "Come, Pagan, are you so unaccustomed to good fortune that you'd cast it away when it's dropped into your lap?"

"Something's wrong."

"Aye, something's wrong," Colin said, at last tearing his attention away from the three maids to focus on Pagan. "You've lost your wits."

"Have I? Or am I right to suspect there may be a serpent in this garden?"

Colin's eyes narrowed wickedly. "The only *serpent* is the one writhing beneath your sword belt, Pagan."

Maybe Colin was right. It was difficult to think straight when his braies were strained to bursting. "Tell me again, what exactly did Boniface say?"

Pagan never rode onto a field of combat blind. It was what had kept him alive through a score of campaigns. Two days earlier he'd sent Boniface, his trusted squire, in the guise of a jongleur, to learn what he could about Rivenloch. It was Boniface who had alerted them to the daughters' intention to bathe in the pond this morn.

Colin rubbed thoughtfully at his chin, recounting what the squire had reported. "He said the lord's wits are addled. He has a weakness for dice, wagers high, and loses often. And, oh, aye," he seemed to suddenly remember. "He said the old man keeps no steward. He apparently intends to pass the castle on to his eldest daughter."

"His *daughter*?" This was news to Pagan.

Colin shrugged. "They're Scots," he said, as if that would explain it all.

Pagan furrowed his brow in thought. "With Stephen claiming the English throne, King David needs strong forces to command the Border lands," he mused, "not *wenches*."

Colin snapped his fingers. "Well, that's it, then. Who better to command Rivenloch than the illustrious Sir Pagan? 'Tis known far and wide that the Cameliard

knights have no peer." Colin turned, eager to get back to his spying.

In the pond below, the voluptuous wench playfully shook her head, spattering her giggling sister and jiggling her weighty breasts in a manner that made Pagan instantly iron hard. Beside him, Colin groaned, whether in bliss or pain, he wasn't sure.

Suddenly realizing the significance of that groan, Pagan cuffed him on the shoulder.

"What's that for?" Colin hissed.

"That's for leering at my bride."

"Which one's your bride?"

They both returned their gazes to the pool.

Pagan would be forever appalled at the lapse of his warrior instincts at that moment. But by the time he heard the soft footfall behind him, it was too late to do anything about it. Colin never heard it at all. He was too busy feasting his eyes. "Wait. I see only two now. Where's the blonde?"

Behind him, a feminine voice said distinctly, "Here."

About the Author

I'm a *USA Today* bestselling author of swashbuckling action-adventure historical romances, mostly set in Scotland, with over a dozen award-winning books published in six languages.

But before my role as a medieval matchmaker, I sang in *The Pinups,* an all-girl band on CBS Records, and provided voices for the MTV animated series *The Maxx,* Blizzard's *Diablo* and *Starcraft* video games, and *Star Wars* audiobooks.

I'm the wife of a rock star (if you want to know which one, contact me) and the mother of two young adults. I do my best writing on cruise ships, in Scottish castles, on my husband's tour bus, and at home in my sunny southern California garden.

I love transporting readers to a place where the bold heroes have endearing flaws, the women are stronger than they look, the land is lush and untamed, and chivalry is alive and well!

I'm always delighted to hear from my readers, so please feel free to email me at glynnis@glynnis.net. And if you're a super-fan who would like to join my inner circle, sign up at http://www.facebook.com/GCReadersClan, where you'll get glimpses behind the scenes, sneak peeks of works-in-progress, and extra special surprises!

CPSIA information can be obtained
at www.ICGtesting.com
Printed in the USA
BVHW03s1849290718
522958BV00001B/66/P